WITH MY LITTLE EYE

WITH MY LITTLE EYE

Gerald Hammond

This first world edition published 2011
in Great Britain and in the USA by
SEVERN HOUSE PUBLISHERS LTD of
9–15 High Street, Sutton, Surrey, England, SM1 1DF.
Trade paperback edition first published
in Great Britain and the USA 2012 by
SEVERN HOUSE PUBLISHERS LTD

British Library Cataloguing in Publication Data

Hammond, Gerald, 1926-
  With my little eye.
  1. Surveyors–Fiction. 2. Housing developers–Fiction.
  3. Police–Scotland–Edinburgh–Fiction. 4. Apartment
  Dwellers–Crimes against–Fiction. 5. Murder–
  Investigation–Fiction. 6. Edinburgh (Scotland)–Fiction.
  7. Detective and mystery stories.
  I. Title
  823.9'14-dc22

ISBN-13: 978-0-7278-8093-2 (cased)
ISBN-13: 978-1-84751-377-9 (trade paper)

All Severn House titles are printed on acid-free paper.

Severn House Publishers support The Forest Stewardship Council [FSC],
the leading international forest certification organisation. All our titles that
are printed on Greenpeace-approved FSC-certified paper carry the FSC logo.

MIX
Paper from
responsible sources
FSC
www.fsc.org   FSC® C018575

Typeset by Palimpsest Book Production Ltd.,
Falkirk, Stirlingshire, Scotland.
Printed and bound in Great Britain by
MPG Books Ltd., Bodmin, Cornwall.

Dedication

I owe to a passing remark the fact that I have spent thirty happy years of nominal retirement in a Scottish village. While visiting one of my sons I called at the local library for a visitor's ticket (of course), and gave the librarian my name. She said, 'Would that be Gerald Hammond the novelist?' and I thought, Here I could be happy. And so I have been. Thus, at the age of 86 and with my doctor issuing ominous warnings about my heart, I feel that I should dedicate this book, almost certainly my last, to the ladies in the Aboyne Library, who have always helped me greatly in finding facts or references.

I would also like to thank Macmillan (editor Hilary Hale nee Watson), who gave me a starting shove and Severn House who allowed me to diverge from crime fiction and write (among two dozen other books) my three favourites, *Fine Tune, Into The Blue* and *The Outpost,* each about people rather than their naughty deeds. Also Anna Telfer, now Editorial Director of Severn House, who has patiently guided my footsteps along the riverbank and accepted without argument my often peevish objections to the copy-editor's assaults, as no other publisher has done. Anna also paid me the compliment of remembering me from a previous incarnation.

Finally I would like to thank every reader who ever wrote to say that they enjoyed one of my books (I have tried to answer each of them, even the Australian lady). I forgive the writer of the one anonymous letter that I ever received, from a lady (I presume) in Liverpool who objected to some of the language that my late friend Earl Bell introduced when I asked him to help me to translate some of the dialogue into Texan. They do talk like that. I feel that when one gets anonymous letters one has arrived.

ONE

'**B**uggah!' said Douglas Young aloud. He then chided himself silently, not for the use of bad language but because a six-year sojourn in an English public school had imposed over his mild, native, southern Scots voice the sort of accent that he was trying to shake off. It raises the hackles and the blood pressure of the diehard Scot whose ancestors have too often been imposed on by men with such accents. The original oath, however, had been provoked only because his feet had led him into an opening that turned out to be neither a neglected B-road nor a well maintained farm road, but the driveway to a substantial house that he had never known existed.

Underwood House stands in the busy, flat and fertile stretch of land lying between the Firth of Forth and the Pentland Hills. It is not far from Edinburgh and only a mile or two from the nearest small town.

Douglas read the name carved into one of the stone gate pillars and sensed puzzlement. Wood, yes. But 'under'? The house lies in woodland which in turn is surrounded by undulating farmland.

The house was built for a minor industrialist during the Scottish shale-oil boom, but when Douglas Young (no relation to the James 'Paraffin' Young who had triggered that boom in the first place) came across the house its state was rather neglected. Douglas was not looking for a house at the time; he was accompanied by Rowan and carrying a shotgun. Nor was he looking for the betrayer of his daughter. Rowan was a black Labrador retriever and, with the permission of the farmer and landowner, they were looking for any unwary rabbit or wood pigeon or, perhaps with luck, a pheasant wandered from a nearby estate and just come into season by a day or two. It would probably be one of last year's birds and tough as an old boot, but with even more luck it might be a hen pheasant released from the laying pens once the duty of laying eggs was done, in which case it might be both large and tender. His involuntary oath had escaped because he had missed a comparatively easy wood pigeon clattering out of the tree-tops. No wood pigeon is very easy but that one should have been less difficult than the average.

Curiosity led his feet to the pillared front doorway.

The front door of the house stood open. A visitor, a general practice surveyor, was inspecting the house on behalf of the owner. He was known to Douglas who, although he was a member of the same profession, worked for a different firm. The two had dined together on professional occasions or exchanged drinks rather more often when winding down after difficult meetings. They examined the property together.

The interior of the house was well laid out with some very handsome rooms. It happened that Douglas had arrived by way of the main drive from which there was no view of the frontage, the leaves still being on the trees. The simple, Georgian-style elevation should have been impossible to spoil but the original designer had managed that feat by means of some regrettable changes to the proportions that had become established for such houses over many years. If Douglas had studied the exterior at this early stage he might have lost interest – which would have been a pity. The house was surrounded by a strip of garden, now running to seed, but at no point could the viewer retreat to view it from further than he could have kicked a football; and the extra material that had spoiled the proportions had been used to add strength and durability to the components. It was robust rather than elegant. Built of weathered stone and roofed with blue-black slates, several Virginia creepers were still glowing vividly against the walls. Douglas could only admire.

As they walked round, it became ever clearer to Douglas that the house would lend itself to division into at least four really excellent apartments with perhaps a fifth, a granny-flat, in the semi-basement.

His companion let slip that the present owner was anxious to sell, and to sell quickly in order to finance an investment abroad. The house was not suitable for a small hotel or large enough for a hostel or a hospice. There was, as usual, an economic depression in Scotland and the larger private house without a sporting estate attached was not selling well. A bed-and-breakfast does not command a high price. An offer of or close to the asking price might well be accepted by return of post.

Douglas was tired of being a wage slave. He was adequately paid but he had an eye for the defects in a property, an instinct for property values and the patience to prepare a thorough report. Clients, he knew, came to his employers' firm because of his work. He also knew that this work was charged out with an oncost that made him feel like weeping. A move into becoming a property developer suddenly seemed very attractive.

The first and most obvious snag was that a property developer needs capital. Considering his assets, Douglas was forced to the conclusion that he had few if any. His car had been more expensive than he could justify even to himself, but it had been in an accident which would make it difficult to sell. He owned most of his flat in Morningside but it was small and dark and without parking space. The rest of his worldly goods might add up to a thousand on a good day, or perhaps double that figure if he threw in his two shotguns, which he had no intention of doing. His bank account would barely sustain him until his next salary cheque.

The next step was to visit his bank manager. After some rather unsatisfactory interviews had taken place at both his bank and at several building societies, it was confirmed that, in a time of recession, a customer without either funds or a long history of borrowing and repayment would have more chance of winning the lottery than of borrowing more than a fraction of the sum required. The lottery proving unforthcoming, he was left with the possibility of a private loan. His mind turned towards Seymour McLeish.

TWO

Attitudes vary remarkably according to how much money the other person has or is believed to have. The pauper sees every well-heeled passer-by as arrogant, condescending and probably a crook, while the rich man sees the pauper as jealous, idle and lacking any ounce of get-up-and-go.

Seymour McLeish had suddenly acquired wealth in mid-life when a novel that he had written during a holiday in Benidorm had hit the best-seller lists, been serialized on television and then made into a prodigiously successful film. Nobody had anticipated such success so an agent on his behalf had negotiated a very favourable contract. He never wrote another word but, as he said, why should he? Douglas had known him at the time of his success but had been unable to detect any change in attitude. Seymour remained just the same vague, untidy, likeable man. He continued to run and even to expand his garage-cum-filling-station and its agency for new and used cars with modest efficiency although, with his film being dubbed into language after language and being repeated regularly on television, he could well have afforded to retire in some comfort.

It was several years since he and Douglas had belonged to the same clay pigeon shooting club. At that time he must have been nearly fifty while Douglas was still in his late twenties. Despite the difference in their ages they had got on well enough that they would still meet occasionally for a pint in their local pub on occasional weekend evenings, but Douglas, on obtaining his qualification and a job, had changed his digs to be nearer his work and each had rather lost interest in breaking inanimate targets.

Douglas diverged from his shortest way home after work the next day and took to well-remembered streets that brought him to a brightly lit forecourt on a main artery where traffic was filtering westward out of Edinburgh. The autumn day had turned foul and a mist thrown up by wet tyres hung over the road. The workshop was closed but the part-time staff, wives of Seymour's mechanics, were busily accepting payment for petrol and diesel. The showroom and offices were still busy. Seymour was in his office, supposedly signing the day's mail, but it was a measure of his alertness that he recognized Douglas's BMW and came out to meet him before he'd finished topping up.

'Well, here's a face I haven't seen for a long while,' Seymour said in his typically cheery manner.

They shook hands. 'Would you have time for a visit to the pub?' Douglas asked. He knew this man would appreciate him cutting to the chase immediately.

Seymour glanced at his watch, reflected for a moment and then shook his head. 'Sorry,' he said. 'Can't. Betty fixed something up and she wants me home by eight without fail.'

'There's something I want to show you,' Douglas explained and hoped he implied a certain amount of enticement into his tone to pique Seymour's interest. 'An hour or two on Sunday afternoon might be better.'

Seymour looked at him speculatively, but Douglas had never been one to waste anybody's time. He nodded and smiled. 'I could manage that.'

'I'll pick you up around two thirty. You're still at the same place?'

Seymour's smile flickered for a fraction of an instant. Douglas was satisfied. Seymour was still in the flat in which his family had been raised. It was convenient to his business, but, that said, he would have run out of favourable comments.

*   *   *

By the Sunday afternoon the sunshine had made a return. Douglas drew the little sports BMW to a halt on the dot of two thirty. On a fine, autumn day he would usually have been running with the top down but he wanted to take some soundings while they travelled.

Seymour's flat was only two storeys up but they were two very high storeys. Douglas was bracing himself for the formidable climb when Seymour emerged from the building, rotund, cheerful and balding, and settled into the passenger seat. 'We rebuilt this for you, didn't we?'

'And very soundly too.'

'I was waiting for an enquiry from your insurers but it never came.'

'I wasn't covered. The damage happened while I was competing in a piddling little rally,' Douglas said bitterly, 'so they turned me down. My policy excluded any sort of competition.'

'Expensive!'

'Very.' As though the subject was still too painful to pursue, Douglas changed it; but he had already made his point. And they were already out of Edinburgh. 'How are Betty and the children?'

'Betty's fine,' Seymour said. 'But lay off the talk of children. Geraldine's nineteen now and Harry isn't far behind. Either of them would eviscerate you if they heard themselves referred to as a child. It must be three or four years since you've seen them.'

'I suppose it must. Are they still at home?'

'Geraldine is. Harry goes to boarding school but he's with us for every holiday. Gerry's still looking for a mission in life.'

Douglas remained hopeful. The flat had always seemed too small for the couple plus two children plus their own friends and the children's friends. Betty had always complained about the lack of storage.

'Did you never find anything more suitable?' Douglas queried.

'Every so often.' Seymour answered and sighed heavily, misting his half of the windscreen. 'But if I didn't hate it, Betty did. One was almost perfect and in just the right place but it didn't have any garden at all. I can't live,' Seymour said plaintively, 'if I don't have some private outdoor space to be eccentric in.'

Douglas hid his amusement. Seymour was the least eccentric person that he knew.

Seymour seemed to sense it. 'It's not that I want to be eccentric,' he said. 'It's just that it would be nice to know that I could be if I wanted to.'

Douglas turned in at the gates. 'That seems reasonable,' he said. 'And I think that this might be the very place.'

THREE

Douglas's guess that Seymour McLeish would be keen turned out to be an underestimate. Spring is usually the optimal time for showing off a property but if the weather is kind a colourful autumn day is as good. Confronted for the first time by the prospect of generous accommodation in rural surroundings, within easy reach of his business, he was enthralled. His wife, fetched in haste that same afternoon to view the potential, had less eyes for old stonework, gracious rooms and lush country-side and was more taken with the possibilities for cupboards galore, some of them heated, and for space not overlooked by many critical or envious neighbours. Seymour would have written a cheque on the spot.

Douglas was only too well aware that building projects not large enough to attract and hold the interest of major contractors may safely be expected to take longer than for ever. It was a shock to his system when he found that the project was rushing ahead, apparently under its own momentum.

Seymour was able to offer inducements, such as immediate attention to a mechanical problem, a jump up the queue for the newest model or a very fair trade-in value. In this manner he found Harris Benton, a young architect in the employ of the Regional Council, who was persuaded to transfer Douglas's sketches into working drawings and to blast them through the processes for official approval. In similar manner, small contractors were persuaded to prepare keen tenders in a very short time and then to live up to the rash promises that had been extracted.

Seymour also found a Mrs Jamieson, a grass widow

whose husband was on contract in the Middle East. The Jamiesons' house had become subject to a not ungenerous Compulsory Purchase Order so that the disproportionately large garden could be added to several others for the benefit of one of the local universities, to form a site for a much needed hall of residence. She visited Seymour's garage in search of a car spacious enough to carry her growing family around and left in a two-year-old hybrid people carrier that the previous owner, a mechanical engineer blessed with considerable ingenuity, before he succumbed to a fatal heart attack, had converted to run on natural gas between its bouts of running on electricity. She also found that she had promised to come and look at Underwood House.

Mrs Jamieson was a down-to-earth woman, handsome rather than beautiful, with a rich head of auburn hair and a conspicuous beauty spot beside her mouth. Her figure was definitely *de luxe*. She dressed to be comfortable, regardless of style or fashion, and yet never looked dowdy. She claimed that she could still get into her wedding dress though nobody had dared to challenge her on the point. She was brisk in manner and well able to take a decision which she was absolutely certain her husband would endorse.

When she made the promised visit to meet Seymour at the house a few days later, he was surprised to note how philosophically she accepted the CPO. 'It's been a good family home to us,' she said, 'but the house will soon be too small and the garden was always too big. Frankly, it's got beyond me and do you know how much a private gardener can get away with charging per hour these days? If they've decided to pay us enough to set up somewhere else with a communal garden, why should I object to a hundred students a year getting a comfortable hall of residence on those sites? My only worry is finding the right place soon enough and not having to make do with a temporary second best which would probably turn out to be a permanency.'

She looked around her at Underwood House. 'You know, I think we've found it,' she exclaimed with a satisfied smile.

It chanced that Harris Benton and Douglas were also on site at the time of her visit. The opportunity for an impromptu committee discussion was too good to miss. It soon became clear that the families represented would fit almost perfectly into the accommodation available.

The main entrance doors to Underwood House gave onto a generous hallway and a wide semicircular staircase which circled round a fat central column which contained the flue from the central heating boiler. Behind and below the stair was a large, old fashioned kitchen with several small sculleries, larders and preparation rooms. It happened that kitchens were the one area in which each participant was determined to *gang their ain gait*. The original kitchen, though arranged for a single house-hold, had been sensibly fitted out and was backed by an attractive garden room. Douglas was only too well aware of the explosive mixture created by more than one woman to a kitchen, but the ladies of the proposed occupancy were remarkably like-minded. There was a general anxiety to get the initial stage of the work completed so that they could gain occupation and set about creating their individual kitchens.

The contentious area of central heating was agreed with surprising ease. The house had recently been piped for new radiators. The old boiler was uneconomic but a new and frugal balanced flue boiler was installed, the running cost to be shared in proportion to a formula devised by Douglas to which nobody objected – largely because nobody else understood it. Everyone breathed again.

On that basis the allocations were agreed. Mrs Jamieson was well suited with the larger ground-floor apartment, which would allow her family a room apiece and give them quick and easy access to the garden. The thunder of little feet would thus not be transmitted to downstairs neighbours.

Mrs Jamieson had difficulty finding child minders for her diverse and growing family (she was becoming noticeably pregnant again) so the next discussion was held at her old house a week later. Douglas had had time to estimate the values of any properties to be sold and of any grants applicable; and a contractor who owed Harris Benton a favour had put some figures on the costs of the work – exclusive of decoration and kitchens, which would be left to each occupier.

Douglas had seen enthusiasm for comparable projects evaporate when discussion of money came to the fore but, perhaps because in each case comparison between the cost of the new and the value of the old had proved very satisfactory, momentum was increasing. He was gratified to be appointed to conduct the sales of the now superfluous properties.

Colour charts and swatches of wallpaper and carpet had already made their appearance and a designer and installer of kitchen fitments was offering to bring samples and brochures. It was high time to remind the purchasers that they did not have any of the necessary consents.

'But we'll get them,' Mrs Jamieson said. The arrival of her third son had not in the least reduced her enthusiasm. 'Why wouldn't we? We're not planning anything that anyone could possibly object to, we're rescuing a piece of heritage that might otherwise fall derelict. There's something else even more important. What about the fourth unit? Bottom right as you look at it, across the hall from me. I know it's the least valuable of the lot if you don't count the granny flat, but we won't want it standing empty.'

'Of course not,' Douglas said. 'But we're hardly started and three-quarters of our quality accommodation's spoken for already. I was waiting to see who turned up.'

'Well, I think he's turned up already. He's a professor of Urban Studies but I think that urban life has been getting him down. He wants to rusticate for a while.'

'Any children?' Douglas asked. He tried not to sound suspicious but Mrs Jamieson was forcing him to remember that couples can multiply. He did not want to live in a mixed sex St Trinian's.

'He's not married and not likely to be.' Mrs Jamieson said casually. She raised her firm bosom against any criticism that might follow. 'He has a partner. A male partner. He's what they call gay. But not a transvestite or anything like that,' she added hastily. 'In fact, you'd never know except that they're quite open about it. Inseparable but not openly affectionate, just the way that gay couples should be – and the other kind too.'

Douglas wondered how, in that case, Mrs Jamieson came to know that a discreet same-sex couple was an item. Her exposition seemed to include several contradictions in terms but he decided not to pursue the matter. There was a tense little silence while each balanced the pros against the cons and decided that the pros had it.

'We'll have to meet again next week. See if he can come then,' Douglas said. 'Better still, both of them. And I've been thinking that however well we may get on with each other now there may be occasions in the future . . .'

Seymour had been a silent listener up until now, nodding his agreement as each point was made, but he spoke up almost for the first time. 'I've been thinking along the same lines. We wouldn't want some co-owner to grab for the best offer he could get and sell to. We could find ourselves with a rock group in our midst.'

'Or worse,' said Douglas. He hoped not to be asked what would be worse. 'We need something along the lines of an American condominium contract whereby general approval is required of a proposed purchaser. I'll dig something out and frame a version that will stand up under Scots law.'

They met again the following week. This time Professor Cullins was present, a small but bustling man in his forties, and he had brought his partner, one Hubert Campion. They were present together, not defiantly but in a gesture of openness. Neither man was noticeably macho nor effeminate, although Campion did have a neat little beard. The professor, unusually for one of his sort, was inclined to pepper his sentences with minor swear words, principally 'bloody', in lieu of adjectives. Apart from this, their manner did not invite criticism or approval and neither was offered; but during conversation it was clear that they were looking forward to setting up home where their orientation seemed likely to be accepted or ignored.

Douglas's draft of the condominium agreement was subjected to a little nit-picking but was universally approved. A solicitor was chosen to prepare deeds. Douglas compiled a final list of the required work for Harris Benton to apply for permits and to seek quotations.

'One last topic,' Douglas said. 'But it's an important one. The original semi-basement kitchen ancillaries – sculleries, pantries and so forth, along with the servants' room – can make a small two-person flat or a generous single-person one. I had it in mind to find a gardener, possibly retired, who would be satisfied with a cheap or free tenancy in exchange for keeping the gardens. I enjoy sitting in a well-kept garden, but I definitely do not enjoy using muscles that I never use for anything else to keep a garden that everyone else will enjoy just as much as I do. Unless one of you . . .?'

There was a sudden interest in the ceiling or in what lay outside the window.

'I thought not. Well, it will be more effective and cheaper to have a permanent gardener and split the cost four ways than to hire individual gardeners by the day. There's not much alteration work to be done in the house, because the flatlet that I'm suggesting would include the present cloakroom, which only needs a shower cubicle added. I've said all this before and it seemed to be generally agreed in principle, except that nobody has yet put forward the name of a suitable candidate. The gardens are in danger of getting out of control, so either we must organize some working parties or we'll have to levy a standing charge to cover the cost of employing a landscaping firm.'

Silence can convey a multitude of emotions. This one made it clear that neither time nor funds were going to be in ample enough supply for either option to be favoured.

The professor spoke up first. He had a mellifluous voice and seemed to enjoy using it. 'Will you leave it in my hands for one more week? The university's deputy head gardener is reaching the bloody retirement age and he might be glad to take it on.'

'Please God,' said Mrs Jamieson. 'But, Professor, why did you have to say "bloody"? You are, presumably, an educated man.'

The professor showed surprise. 'The sentence,' he said, 'would not have scanned so well. Rhythm is important in the spoken word.'

From then on Douglas examined the professor's utterances and, sure enough, most of them scanned better for the insertion of a modicum of vulgarity. He toyed with the idea of rounding off the rhythm of his own words in the same vein but decided that he had quite enough difficulty filtering out his Englishness.

FOUR

P reparations for work often take longer than the work itself but for once, while the prospective occupiers, the favoured contractor and the various suppliers and subcontractors were champing at their respective bits, the processes of approvals and tendering hurried along their predestined paths.

Even the processes of selling the now superfluous houses went with such speed that the Jamiesons in particular found themselves in danger of being homeless. The Scottish custom of inviting offers for a property and then waiting until enough purchasers have expressed interest may (or may not) ultimately extract the best price for the seller, but a buyer may miss a whole succession of houses by a tiny margin and have to pay a solicitor and a surveyor in respect of each of them. Douglas priced the properties high but on a fixed price basis and they sold quickly.

This turned out to have a valuable spin-off. With the threat of eviction on one hand and the offer of her removal expenses as an inducement on the other, Mrs Jamieson moved her whole family and all its trappings into the rooms where her apartment was to be created, with the intention of camping there. Happily the area included one of the spacious existing bathrooms. The original kitchen, to be shared initially, was still in working order.

By chance the house was visited that same night by a party of thieves presumed to be after lead pipes and roofing. The Jamiesons' wolfhound, however, had already developed a sense of territory and exploded into action. The thieves made off in great haste but omitted the use of their van's lights, probably for fear of revealing a registration number. The result was a glancing blow to a tree, leaving paint traces. Between the damage to the van and the incompetence of the men, the police had little difficulty tracking them down. Thereafter, Underwood House was off the map of lawbreakers.

The final occupier, proposed by the professor, was Stan Eastwick, a gnarled but jovial-looking old man who had been second-in-command of the university's gardens and greenhouses for more years than anyone cared to remember. He was very active despite developing a pot belly that necessitated much work on his part with needle and thread before off-the-peg clothes would accommodate themselves to his proportions. He had remained single although rumour had it that he had been a bit of a dog in his day. He had stalwartly refused to occupy accommodation provided by the university but had purchased a modest but now quite valuable flat. He decided to sell his flat and buy the granny flat that was being assembled from the pantries and sculleries of the house; and he was given a favourable price on the written understanding that the gardens would be his responsibility. He was already well provided with gardening tools and machinery. Rumours as vague but as insistent as those about his past life suggested that he had acquired his equipment by retaining and reconditioning machines that were believed to be clapped out and had been replaced at his employer's expense, but he was prepared to swear that every last trowel or trug was legitimately his own. The other householders turned a blind eye.

His retirement date was still several months off, which allowed time for the necessary alterations to the building but, apparently on the principle of 'one year seed, seven years weed', he began work on the gardens in his leisure time. He was also a valuable general handyman, capable of polished workmanship in joinery or electrics. When a defect was uncovered in the original structure or some essential small work had not been thought of at the time

of the original quotations, Stan could usually turn his hand
to it or he had a friend who could. It was Douglas's experience that whatever was added to an existing contract usually
brought with it a disproportionate share of the oncosts and,
unless the contractor was unusually amenable, it was often
safer to keep such work separate.

The fabric of the building being in good repair, the
building works required were mostly the opening or closing
up of doorways and windows, some moving of partitions
and the creation of one new bathroom. Harris Benton, after
some research, had come up with a floor finish that could
be counted on to muffle to a large extent the passage of
noise down through the floors and that work turned out to
be the most expensive but also the most worthwhile part
of the contract. That particular task suffered delay because
occupiers were already making a start to the decoration
and the moving in of furniture, but constant liaison made
sure that the appropriate owners, or others on their behalves,
were on the spot to transfer furniture and packing cases
out of the way. The subcontractor and his men proved
adaptable; and almost amicable compromises were soon
reached over cost and delay. Douglas, like Mrs Jamieson,
soon decided to move in and let the men work round him,
so he was always available to lend a hand or to suggest a
compromise. The day appointed for the new owners to
take occupation passed with hardly a stir because much of
it had already occurred. Only six months had passed since
Douglas had found the place, but spring had brought new
hope and impetus.

FIVE

Almost on schedule the paint and paper dried, the dust settled and by general agreement one Sunday afternoon was declared to have something akin to a proper Sabbath calm. Douglas had been pacifying any argumentative tradesman with a promise that when all was finished there would be a celebration; this was usually countered by the observation that such promises were frequently given but never honoured. It was not to be expected that everyone would be free to assemble at the same time, but most of the future occupants and some of their friends, along with the more popular of the builders' tradesmen, managed to put in at least a token appearance. Douglas had pressured the proprietor of a wine shop to signify his appreciation of a satisfactory price negotiated for the purchase of his premises by the contribution of a few bottles of a tolerable Rhine wine, while most of those who came brought rather more than they expected to consume for fear of being thought mean by their new neighbours. The result was a table with a formidable stack of bottles.

Some parties may be planned months ahead and still fall flat; others may occur almost spontaneously and burst into life of their own accord; and this was one of the latter sort. At the end of a period of hard work and financial anxiety, of the kind in which any surprise is almost certainly unwelcome, the relief of finishing with even a little time and money in hand left the residents ill prepared to make use of either. The builders' tradesmen, by invitation, had brought their wives or lady friends to see a job in which they took some pride, but Douglas suspected that part of the motivation was to let wives see that quite respectable and responsible people might move into accommodation that still lacked that final decoration.

The chosen venue was the (temporarily) communal kitchen, which had been enlarged to include the garden room and was for the moment doubling up as a dining room, which had been added to the house by the last owner. It was now furnished comfortably but discordantly with all the cast-offs of the various occupants. The previous owners of the house had entertained lavishly so the room was large. Douglas's tentative suggestion of a get-together around mid afternoon, in order to get to know each other and to decide a few minor management points, resulted in Hilda Jamieson and Betty McLeish, who had lingered after lunch to share the washing up and have a good gossip, fetching their own contributions to the festivities and starting the party. In the mysterious way by which news of free drink spreads, the other members of the enlarged household, their volunteer helpers and favoured members of the building team came trickling in. Conversation became general and loud. There was laughter.

It was soon clear that the group was unusually free from jealousy and hostilities – with one non-human exception. Mrs Jamieson's deerhound had already decided that this was his territory and his pack. Rowan, being black, did not easily communicate friendship or submission but peace of a sort had become established. Stan Eastwick, however, had a bulldog bitch. Winnie was of a peaceable nature, but a flat face and a docked tail form other barriers in the way of peaceful communication. Bloodshed seemed imminent.

The most obvious solution would have been to banish the opponents to their respective homes; but living under the same roof they would be bound to meet. Douglas, hoping one day to achieve the perfect gundog, took his dog training seriously and devoured every publication on the subject. Having been inclined to broadcast advice or even to pontificate on the subject he had clearly elected himself to deal with any canine attitude problems before they became established. The aggressive signals coming from the wolfhound, and especially the deep-throated rumblings, were ominous enough to make the hairs crawl up the back of his neck, but he persevered and with Mrs Jamieson restraining and soothing her wolfhound, the signs of violence, the white-rimmed eyes and the stiff-legged posture with the weight on the forefeet, began to abate while Stan Eastwick calmed and reassured his bulldog until the more noticeable signals of peaceful intent – yawning, lip-licking and blinking – were accepted.

Douglas's reputation as a useful person to have around was enhanced, more so when the three dogs were later seen hunting rabbits together through the buddleia bushes.

The end of hostilities was the signal for another round of drinks. Douglas had been acting as host and barman, duties that anchored him at the mercy of the grateful dog-owners; but Stan now seemed to have volunteered for this role and Douglas was able to slip away and chat for a minute with Mrs Jamieson. That lady was for once not plagued by children. Douglas asked her where all her brood had gone.

'They're in front of the television,' she said cheerfully.

That caught his attention. Many parents dislike seeing their children taking root before the box. 'Do you let them watch as much as they like?'

'We have an inflexible rule. They watch the documen-taries on SKY, the historical ones and wildlife and how the universe works and so on. And politics, of course. After that, they can watch whatever they like for the same duration on mainstream TV. You should see them arguing over the *TV Times.*'

'I think that that's brilliant,' Douglas said. He sometimes felt that he had learned more since getting the Discovery channel than in all his schooldays. 'But have you barred the porn channels?'

She shrugged. 'I dare say that that would be just as educational,' she said. 'But I don't think that they've found them yet.'

The hi-fi was playing a CD of a well known Scottish violinist playing a reel. 'I went to hear her playing that in the Coo cathedral,' said a voice behind Douglas. 'It was a let-down.' He looked round. An angry looking man was standing behind him. He raised his eyebrows.

Mrs Jamieson whispered, 'He's Stan Eastwick's brother.'

Minutes later the TV seemed to have lost its power to captivate and the Jamieson family were to be seen mingling with the guests, monopolizing the conversation after the manner of the young. Douglas found himself confronted by the more attractive form of the eldest of Mrs Jamieson's brood, Natasha, the forward state of whose education was now explained. What might have suggested the outlandish name never emerged; the others of the family were blessed with simple Scottish or biblical names.

Natasha was known in the family, and soon by all the other residents, simply as Tash. She was a genuine redhead with very blue eyes and creamy skin. (Any questions were explained away when Mr Jamieson came home on leave and was observed to have the reddest hair ever seen in the area.) Tash was said to be nineteen years old, but she was taking at least one gap year in preparation for university.

Douglas had previously only seen her in a singularly unflattering school uniform. She had arrived late at the party after walking back from a music lesson in the nearest village and had delayed her entrance while she changed into something more becoming. Mrs Jamieson admitted later that she had realized that Tash, having reached an age for attracting the attention of the opposite sex, could not be segregated indefinitely and instead she had given Tash a very serious lecture, not so much about the birds and bees but more concerning viruses, spermatozoa and the fickleness of men, and had then allowed her to choose her own leisurewear.

The outcome could have been disastrous but in fact it had resulted in a dress in mossy green that flattered her hair colour but also did things for her figure without quite clinging or catching the light. The sheen of nylon did wonders for her already delightful legs. Douglas now saw for the first time that Tash was an exceptionally pretty, not to say beautiful, girl with a sexual attraction that would have made a saint turn his head. His first impulse was to protect her from predatory males by predating her himself. This was followed immediately by a sense of shame and a determination to do something unspecified but very special for her protection.

It also became clear that along with education and intelligence Tash was gifted with a sense of humour. The party was winding down into the peace of a fine evening. The two resident ladies had taken over the cooking end of the kitchen-dining room to begin preparations for an evening meal but others were strolling on the grass.

'You're not married, are you?' Tash asked.

Douglas pushed aside the hope that she asked the question because her interest was in him as a prospective bridegroom. Although he had chosen to make for himself an apartment with three bedrooms and two baths, this had been partly with a view to long-term profit. He had managed to lose some of the extra cost among the general building works although he might have admitted that somewhere at the back of his mind lurked the thought that ladies might be encouraged by the signs of a family-sized house.

To Tash, he admitted his single state and explained that he hoped to need office space in the not too distant future. His tongue was loosened by the wine. 'I was engaged once,' he said, 'but she went . . .' He paused. He had been conscious of the Englishness of his voice making a reappearance where he was not sure that it would be welcomed, and the word 'off' was dangerously close to emerging as 'orf', a serious giveaway. 'She went away with somebody else,' he finished. The story was true though he rarely told it, partly because the betrayal had been rather a relief. That fiancée had been becoming possessive.

Tash was obviously moved. Her very blue eyes were usually clear and bright, the irises flecked with brown and green. Douglas was sure that he could detect a tear. He was in danger of losing the thread of their conversation when Hubert Campion, the professor's companion, fell foul of Harry, Seymour McLeish's son. Harry was at the age to despise absolutely everything, especially a male preoccupation with clothes, and he soon tired of Campion's complaint that certain fabrics were prone to producing little woolly balls. Harry's patience had very soon failed.

'If you talk any more about little woolly balls to me,' he said, 'you'll get a kick in the little woolly balls.' He stalked out of the room, rather pleased with his turn of phrase.

Mrs Jamieson chased after him and her voice could be heard scolding him for his rudeness.

In search of more congenial company, Campion tried Stan Eastwick but soon tired of a long-winded explanation of why he grudged paying VAT on somebody else's work and intended to make use of his own and his brother's skills to finish the fittings and finishes in his flat. Campion transferred his attention and decided to join Tash and Douglas in their duologue.

Douglas consoled himself with the reflection that at least Campion, as a presumed homosexual, should be no danger to Tash; but this was overset by the fact that Campion was suffering from a passing deafness. Having difficulty hearing the words of others he proved quite willing to do the talking. 'I hear my own voice reverberating inside my head,' he said loudly.

'You must find that terribly boring!' Tash said. Douglas masked his amusement at the hidden insult.

'Well, it is,' Campion said. 'My doctor says that there's

no wax in there, it's just that my passages are very narrow.'
(Tash and Douglas avoided each other's eyes.) 'He said
the only treatment was to hold my nose and try to blow
hard, to keep them stretched open.'

This statement reminded Tash of the words of her least
favourite games mistress. She paraphrased. 'Breathe in
through the mouth and out through the ears,' she said.

'It isn't as simple as that,' Campion persisted. 'I can
hear it coming out through my good ear, but the one that
had the mastoid operation . . . nothing.'

Douglas let Tash see him palm a peanut from one of the
dishes. 'Tell your doctor that it needs some attention from
Dyno-rod drain clearance. Of course, it may wear –' he
gathered control of his tongue '– off in a year or two.'
He paused and rearranged his mouth. 'Let's see if we can hear
it,' he suggested.

'You can't see whether you can hear something,' Tash
objected. ''s a contradiction in terms.' She had only been
sipping at a glass or two of wine to which her mother had
turned a blind eye, but her system could not emulate
Douglas's more practiced resistance to alcohol.

'I don't think it's loud enough for anyone else to hear,'
said Campion seriously. He had had his share of the wines
and perhaps a little more.

'Let's try it,' Douglas said. With their eyes, Douglas and
Tash were sharing the emerging foretaste of a joke.

Campion looked unconvinced but he took a grip of his
own nose and blew. His eyes seemed ready to pop. Douglas
put his left ear close to Campion's left. He was looking
past the other man and into Tash's face as she put out the
tip of her tongue and made a farting sound.

Douglas kept his face straight, pulled back his head and
showed Campion the peanut. 'Was this in your ear?'
Douglas asked.

The other seemed uncertain. 'I don't think so,' he said.
'Did you make that noise?' he asked Tash.

Tash was the very picture of wounded innocence. 'Certainly not! What are you suggesting? Do you think I'm the sort of person . . .?'

'Not particularly. Oh my God! What's happening to me?' Campion turned and lurched out of the room.

Tash and Douglas collapsed onto a convenient settee and wept tears of laughter onto each other's shoulders. Her mother watched from the doorway but they had not passed beyond the bounds of propriety.

SIX

The new occupiers of Underwood House had to adjust to changes of company and environment but, once the altered background was accepted, old habits reasserted themselves and life, as is its habit, rolled on its way little changed.

Douglas was gratified to find that some of his employer's earlier clients preferred his more relaxed way of working and had decided to follow him. His reports were not rigidly formal but were slanted to ensure that the client understood the ramifications. He was kept busy. He might have foundered under the weight of divided responsibilities, but, out of the blue, Tash spoke to him.

'You need a typist, telephonist and filing clerkess,' she said. 'They spent ages trying to teach me secretarial skills at school.'

This was interesting. 'Did they succeed?' He had wondered why she had come to breakfast in a businesslike skirt and jumper and with her hair pulled back.

'We have to find out. I think I should spend my gap years as your dogsbody.'

'Could you hold the end of a tape measure?'

She smiled and he thought that she probably did not realize how beguiling her smile was. 'I think that's within my capabilities. And I'm not proud. How about it?'

Douglas was not reticent in agreeing.

The arrangement worked well. She enjoyed the work because it was crisp, factual and responded to a methodical approach. Douglas accepted her because she was cheap, well trained, easy on the eye and biddable. Her mother developed the habit of popping in unexpectedly to ask some question about their flat but never had cause for concern.

The other residents were already embedded in routine.

Seymour McLeish spent most of each weekday at the service and filling station but was happy to socialize in the evenings and weekends. He had chosen his staff well and money was being made for him without stretching him too far.

Geraldine McLeish was of a similar age to Tash and the two were regular companions if not always friends. Geraldine, who acted as cashier and pump attendant at the service station, had no ambition beyond waiting for Mr Right to come along; Tash watched her to be sure that she was not considering Douglas Young in that rosy light.

Hubert Campion, the professor's partner, was also employed by the university as a technician. The university had been plagued by a spate of thefts and a security purge was making inroads into his leisure time. Campion was very often late home for the evening meal. He said, with a sigh, that universities were an easy target for thieves; there were too many faces to remember and nobody walking the quads carrying papers was ever challenged. There was too ready a market for anything containing electronics. Until someone was scared away or caught, computers, microscopes and particularly any electronic gear had to be locked up at night, a duty that fell to the already overburdened technicians such as himself, he said.

In most of the new apartments the fitting out of kitchens was left to one of several specialist firms and the work of decoration went on at its own pace whenever the occupants felt so inclined. Stan Eastwick's flat, however, had been cobbled together, including the original kitchen adjuncts of a scullery, a larder, a laundry room, a coal cellar and other humble holes and corners, and although the building contract had embraced the opening of essential new windows, turning the dark dungeons into comparatively bright little rooms, some brick partitions had to be removed to make rooms of useable size. The dirt and grease of ages had to be scrubbed away and the exposed mess painted or papered over. Stan was also making his own kitchen with fitments purchased from a major DIY supplier. Stan's brother George turned out to have skills as a bricklayer and also at plasterwork. George and Stan virtually lived in what had been the housekeeper's room while the flat developed around them.

The brothers were not dissimilar in appearance but whereas Stan was a quiet but jolly soul his brother was definitely dour. He was easily displeased and always ready to let the world hear about his displeasure. Until his retirement date, Stan still went off to his work at the university each weekday and kept the Underwood House gardens in check in the evenings. (Gardens in the plural is perhaps an overstatement, but there was a spreading rose garden beside the front door and beds of flowering shrubs elsewhere. Grass had been sown in walkways and small lawns around the house and, though summer had not yet arrived, spring temperatures were now high enough for grass to grow and when grass grows it has to be mown. Some of the residents were already talking about croquet and clock golf.)

When his retirement was finalized Stan spent his days overtaking the backlog of gardening work and George was left to interpret Harris Benton's drawings as best he could. At least once, a shouting match between the two brothers penetrated through the special flooring as far as the flat above. As a disinterested observer, but all too often faced with George's glare, Douglas was driven to the conclusion that George was not simply reacting against imagined hostility but was himself full of hate for everybody and everything and so attracting the very real hostility that he had been imagining.

On a Wednesday in April, the silver birches were already fuzzy with infant leaf and the other trees were preparing to follow. Rock plants and alpines were splashing their yellows and purples around the edges of the borders. Girls wore shorter skirts and thinner dresses even though they shivered in the cold.

SEVEN

Douglas and Tash were ignoring the spring sunshine and golden outlook. The two worked well together. They had finished preparing a report and final accounts for the contractors' work at Underwood House. Most of the necessary payments had been made and Seymour's advance repaid. They had switched their attention to reports and valuations of Edinburgh properties for the building society that had fallen out with Douglas's previous employer but liked Douglas's style. Douglas was quietly contented. Rowan was at his feet. In Douglas's mind, a home was not a home without a lovely girl to do his bidding and a Labrador snoring and farting under his chair.

That day, the tranquil flow of work was broken by the arrival of George Eastwick. No visitor was welcome during working hours unless he came bringing more work or money and George brought only the indiscriminate hatred that he incessantly broadcast. However, at least George, who was acutely aware of the value of money, took off his boots before venturing onto new carpets.

Douglas welcomed him with apparent sincerity and indicated a chair. 'George. Good morning, what can I do for you?'

George looked around appreciatively, as well he might. The last occupiers of the house had entertained on a lavish scale and their dining room (over the former kitchen and served by a dumb waiter) was appropriately large and panelled. Douglas, looking towards the day when he hoped to be chairing meetings of a syndicate of investors, had retained it. His desk, vast and ornate and topped with glass over leather, had come out of an auction house at a silly price – it was too big for most offices and there had been some attack by furniture beetle, now eradicated, so that Douglas's bid had been the only one. The glass top was covered with plans and A4 pages.

'I just looked in,' George explained with unusual moderation, 'to ask if you'd seen my brother around.'

Douglas and Tash shook their heads. 'Gone AWOL has he?' Douglas asked, just to break an awkward little silence.

Stan usually had the jolly expression of one of Snow White's happier dwarves as drawn by the Disney studios, but George's face suggested that he could have been perpetually resenting an enquiry after his piles. He was looking even fiercer than usual. 'He said that I hadn't followed the drawing closely and I said that the dimensions on the drawing didn't add up right and he said that that was only because the width of the wee passage wasn't quite the same at one end from the other – it tapers a bittie, you see? Anyway, we fell out and I've not seen him since the beginning of the week.'

'He can't have gone home,' Tash said. 'He got a buyer for his flat and he's moved his things.'

'He has a bit of a reputation,' Douglas said. He glanced dubiously at Tash, wondering how far he should go. 'Perhaps he met a lady.'

'Yon was lang syne,' George said. While Douglas was trying to lose his English accent in order to fit back better into his own country, both the brothers were trying to melt into the university polyglot company that they moved among. When angry or perturbed, George lapsed into his native Scots. Now he drew himself up. 'Changed days,' he said. 'We're older now. And, truth to tell, Stan never stayed more than a night with the same woman. Grudged the expense,' he explained.

That suggested to Douglas that Stan had been in the

habit of paying for his female comforts, a subject best avoided in Tash's company until he could be quite sure of the degree of her enlightenment. 'If we see him we'll remind him to speak to you,' Douglas said.

'Aye.' But George looked even more embittered. 'The hale thing is this. Stan never trusted me. He was fine pleased with the work I did on his wee house and the price I let him awa' wi'. It went back to something that happened when we were boys, but I'll not go into that except to say that Stan wouldn't let me through his house, just the bittie I was working on and the bit we were living in. Maybe he had secrets but more likely he was feared I'd make off with one of his treasures – not that I jalouse he'd have ocht of great value.'

Douglas and Tash exchanged unhappy glances. 'But why are you telling us all this?' Douglas asked.

George recovered a touch of his old bellicosity. 'I'm just explaining if you'll let me finish. Now I'm just feared that something may have come over Stan. He could have had a fit, maybe, or an accident and be needing help. I telled him his locks are as common as fleas on a hedgehog but he wouldn't listen. I could go into any of his rooms and that's what I'll do but I want somebody with me – a witness to say that I didn't touch a thing. And if it's you that's with me you can tell him if what I've done is in reasonable accord with the drawings.'

It seemed an unusual request and Douglas was reluctant to break off while his own work was going well. 'That wouldn't prove that you hadn't been in there on some other occasion,' he pointed out.

'I ken that damned fine,' snapped George. 'I'm not bloody daft.' He stopped and produced a lopsided smile that sat badly on his irritable features. 'Look, will you do me this wee favour or will you not?'

'I suppose so. Give me a couple of minutes.' Douglas turned his eyes to Tash, to his own relief. There could be no doubt which of them gave more pleasure to the eye. 'Tash, type it up in draft as far as we've got and then make a start to setting up a decimal filing system the way I showed you. I'll be back. Come on, then,' he said to George.

EIGHT

S tan's flat was to be the only one with its own entrance
door which had been the original back door and
tradesmen's entrance. They left Douglas's flat and
descended the imposing rubber-covered staircase into the
hall. All was clean and polished, showing the pride
the ladies were taking in the new premises. Two connections
between the house and the original servants' quarters
had been blocked off, so they left the house by the front
door, between a pair of Ionic columns supporting a pedi-
ment that gave shelter to a waiting visitor. After working
steadily at the desk for hours the sunshine came as a
pleasant shock. Douglas drew in deep draughts of the fresh
air. A gravel path led round the gable of the house to where
a secondary drive, little more than a gravel farm track,
arrived at the back of the house. The lower window panes
of the semi-basement flat were mostly of reeded glass, to
give servants and employers privacy from each other, so
that it was impossible to look for Stan that way.

The back door was standing open and George led the
way down the seven steps and inside.

During the planning stages, Douglas had of necessity
been familiar with what the visitor might have regarded
as the secret intestines of the house. Being semi-basement
they had been dark, cramped and unattractive and they had
smelled of cheap soap. The improvement had not yet trans-
formed them but it had begun. The whole area was cleaner
and, after some brick partitions had been removed, more
open. New plasterwork shone white and both paint and
paper had begun to give life to the blank surfaces. Douglas
experienced the inevitable designer's jolt at seeing his

vision beginning to emerge full size. The vision was still impaired by all the half executed alterations and the paraphernalia of decoration that still dominated the space. The smell of paint was everywhere. They ducked under a platform that spanned between two stepladders.

Stan's bulldog bitch, Winnie, rushed to meet them, the picture of canine relief mingled with uncertainty. Clearly she was unsure whether to welcome human help and support or to chase away intruders. Deciding that both men were known to her and that there was much more important business awaiting her attention, she bolted out onto the nearest grass and squatted for long overdue relief. Returning, she came to Douglas, rolled over in a gesture of submission and then, rising, hurried to scratch at a brightly painted door. She was drooling slightly.

'When was she last fed?' Douglas asked.

'I've no idea.'

George brought a can of dog-food, still half full, from the fridge and filled two dog-bowls, one with food and the other with water. Winnie was the only being that George ever treated with consideration. Douglas had noticed that the water-bowl was bone dry. Winnie threw herself at the food dish before it quite reached the floor. Douglas felt a hollowness in his own midriff. Something was far wrong. Like many a dog owner, Stan might have neglected himself but never his dog.

George fetched a ring of keys from what was obviously a living room in a near finished state and they began a tour. George was not content to glance into each room to be sure that his brother was not lying on the floor or furniture. He looked into cupboards and wardrobes, pointing out that Stan could easily have collapsed in such a confined space. Douglas began to suspect that George was motivated largely by curiosity.

They were almost back at the entry door when George unlocked and pulled open an oak door giving onto a very short passage. This had been the coal cellar and the new oil-fired balanced flue boiler could be heard whispering from its place where the old boiler had stood, in a tiny compartment behind another door to the right.

But there was no time to admire the more efficient use of space or the neat decoration. A figure sprawled at their feet. Douglas recognized the well-worn cardigan, the corduroys and Stan's thinning grey hair. George started forward, but Douglas, keeping control of all his emotions with an effort, put an arm across to stop him.

'Wait. You wanted a witness and that's what you've got.' Douglas went down on one knee and touched the neck. 'I'm sorry, George. Your brother's dead. There's no pulse.' He pointed silently to the yellow stain where escaping urine had dried on the floor. 'And he's cold and stiffening. It happened some time ago. No wonder the dog was ravenous and desperate for the loo.'

Winnie, the bulldog bitch, tried to push between them but Douglas caught her collar. She whined on a rising scale, a sound that brought home the dread of death more surely than words could have done. On the sad features of the bulldog a greater sadness and the eternal fear for the future could be seen. To a person, the loss of a dog may be a tragedy. To a dog, loss of an owner threatens disaster.

George's face showed less emotion. Nothing is gained by hating the dead. 'What do we do now?' he asked dully.

Douglas thought back to a friend who had broken his neck in a fall downstairs. 'You need a death certificate. Who was his doctor?'

'I don't think that he had een. He was aye healthy was Stan, working outdoors as he did. Should we call an ambulance? And an undertaker?'

Douglas was trying hard to recall what had been said after his friend's death. 'Ambulance, yes. But you can't bring in an undertaker yet. You'll have to let the police know.'

'Police?' George looked dumbfounded. 'What's it to dae with them?'

'When somebody dies in Scotland, if there isn't a doctor to certify natural death, the police report to the procurator fiscal who decides whether or not to call for a fatal accident inquiry. You'd better phone them.'

'Why me?'

'He was your brother,' Douglas pointed out.

'I don't have a phone.'

Douglas's right foot wanted to give George a good kick. This was not the moment for nit-picking. Instead, he produced his slim mobile and offered it to George, who stepped back and hid his hands. 'I couldn't use een o' they things. You make the call.'

It seemed hardly worth arguing about. Douglas keyed the emergency services and asked for the police. More from habit than for any other reason he was careful to keep the Englishness out of his voice – the telephone is notorious for exaggerating accents and the police can be just as prone to Anglophobia as even the French. He was told to wait where he was and that officers were on their way. He remembered to tell the disembodied voice to direct the officers to the back drive. It would have been more comfortable for him to wait upstairs but George seemed reluctant to leave the body, which Douglas supposed showed a certain amount of respect. They sat in folding garden chairs in Stan's living room until the crunch of tyres on gravel told of the arrival of the police at the door.

Douglas decided that he had more than enough to be thinking about, so when George got out of his chair and went to meet the officers he was content to sit where he was. The police contingent comprised a tall young sergeant in plain clothes and a uniformed constable whose duties seemed to include those of chauffeur, note-taker, recording technician and witness. Also, Douglas thought, probably custody officer if police time were being wasted.

The sergeant introduced himself as Detective Sergeant Dodson, the constable remained anonymous. 'Who made the phone call?' the sergeant asked.

Douglas raised his hand. 'I made the call, but the body seems to be that of Mr Stan Eastwick, the owner of this flat. This is his brother George.'

The sergeant looked at him coldly. 'That is not what I asked you. You made the call so you can show me the body. We'll take things in sequence, please.'

As Douglas rose to comply he noticed, from the corner of his eye, George seeming to relax. The constable was left to keep an eye on George while the sergeant followed through to the small passage and stooped over the body. 'You've touched him?'

'Only to check that he was cooling and that there was no pulse.'

'Is that why you didn't call for an ambulance?'

Douglas nodded. 'I guessed that you wouldn't want him moved. He was beyond any help that an ambulance could bring.'

The sergeant nodded, straightening his back. 'You know he's dead and I know he's dead. If he knows anything he knows it too. But in the eyes of the law he's in limbo until he's certified dead. Who was his doctor?'

'So far as I know, he didn't have one.'

The sergeant produced his radio, reported an unexplained death and asked for the attendance of the police surgeon.

'His brother can tell you more that I can,' Douglas said. 'I live and work upstairs and I've got plenty to be getting on with. Shall I get out of your way and wait upstairs? I'll still be available at a moment's notice.'

After a few seconds of silent thought the sergeant said, 'There's only a Transit van outside this door and one car standing at the front.'

'The car's mine, the blue BMW. The van belonged to the dead man. George Eastwick had a terrible old car but it went to the crusher late last week. I've seen George driving the van. I think it was insured for either of them to drive.'

The sergeant absorbed the information without comment. 'Don't go near the van, sir, without asking me first. Yes, go and get on with your own business and I'll get a statement from you later.'

Douglas nodded. Outside, the sunshine looked less cheerful and the cool air was definitely cold. Nobody likes to be reminded of his own mortality and Douglas had other concerns on his mind.

Upstairs, Tash had finished the typing and was struggling to arrange Douglas's files in the way that he had decreed. He called her to him. 'More dictation,' he said. 'I'm afraid Stan Eastwick's dead. We'd better prepare a note for the other householders.'

From his manner, Tash had already guessed that ugly news was coming. She settled without a word and produced her dictation book. Douglas took off an imaginary hat to her. She was going to type the note, so she would hear the facts and so there was no need to waste time asking questions. Douglas liked that. A woman who thought first and spoke afterwards, if at all, was, he thought, a treasure to be prized.

'Do a note for your mother, the professor and Seymour.' And Douglas dictated the following note:

This is to advise you that Stan Eastwick has been found dead today. The cause is not yet known. He did not have a doctor to certify death from natural causes so the police will be making enquiries.

He may be intestate. If anybody knows of a will please tell me or the police. But even if he left a will the most likely legatee will be his brother George.

The deeds do not prevent an owner leaving the

property to a relative. Consideration was given to the possibility of allowing the other occupiers first option on buying back the property but it was not felt that this would stand up in Scots law but was likely to lead to further expensive litigation. It therefore seems probable that George will inherit the basement flat. Stan was given preferential terms in return for undertaking to care for the gardens. It was assumed that we would have some years before we had to concern ourselves with the gardens and the occupancy of the basement flat, by which time many things might have changed. Urgent consideration is suggested. Please try to keep tomorrow evening available for discussion and let me know whether you could be free at, say, 8 p.m. I will try to know more by then.

NINE

Every task that Douglas's clients put his way culminated in a written report, so that the speed and accuracy of Tash's typing had been improving with steady practice. She was already running off copies on the printer when there came the sound of footfalls and not a little puffing from the stairwell. The sergeant, it seemed, had grown unaccustomed to climbing stairs. The doors were standing open. He uttered a wordless but admiring sound when he arrived in the palatial room.

Douglas introduced Tash as his secretary. 'Do you want me to come down again?' he asked. 'You could have phoned.'

The sergeant picked out one of the visitors' chairs, raised his eyebrows politely for permission to sit and finally lowered himself onto one of the mahogany and leather dining chairs that Douglas had claimed and stored after his father died and his mother went into sheltered housing.

'Your presence won't be necessary just now. My colleague is taking down the basic facts as told by the brother of the deceased. We'll have more privacy here. The police surgeon has been and gone.'

Now that he had leisure to notice it, Douglas realized that the sergeant had a lilt that stemmed from the West Highlands.

'Did he say how Stan Eastwick came to die?'

'Nothing so helpful. It's not his job to determine the cause of death,' the sergeant explained. 'If he notices anything relevant he should report it and he should make a record of the body's location, position and condition. But his real *raison d'être* is to certify that the corpse is indeed dead and that we are not sending a still breathing victim to the morgue, which is exactly what he did certify. He also stated that he could see no reason for the sudden death so we will have to have a post-mortem examination. I tell you all this so that you can add it to your – um – news flash if you wish.' With his forefinger the sergeant stirred the copy of Douglas's note that lay on the table almost under his nose. He seemed to have the unusual knack of reading a document upside down while speaking quite lucidly on a different subject. 'We're waiting for the pathologist and it seemed a good opportunity to get your account into the record.'

'We don't have much chance of getting anything else done,' Douglas agreed. 'May Miss Jamieson stay with us?'

'I see no reason why not.' The sergeant produced a large notebook and several ballpoint pens. 'She may even have something to contribute. My colleague has the use of the wire recorder and my shorthand is not great, so we'll take it slowly.'

It was necessary for Douglas to go back and tell briefly the story of the development at Underwood House so that the sergeant could understand the arrival of Stan Eastwick, his unique status among the occupants and also the presence of George.

'Had you had any cause to doubt his state of health?' asked the sergeant.

'None at all. He seemed to be the healthiest man of his age that I ever met. He didn't just die of heart failure then?'

'Everybody dies of heart failure. It just means dying. If you mean heart disease or a heart attack,' the sergeant said severely, 'then say so. But there were no signs of that nature. To the uninitiated – that means me – he seems to have dropped dead for no particular reason, but no doubt the pathologists will find something to explain it. You knew him in life and you saw his body. Did you notice a change in his colour?'

'The light is feeble in that little piece of passage and it has one of those new bulbs that only light up very slowly. I saw enough to recognize him. He looked pale and I thought his lips were blue, which is what made me think of a heart attack. He looked a bit puffy, too.'

The sergeant looked at him. 'But you did recognize him? Clearly enough to be sure that it wasn't another brother?'

'Definitely. Anyway, they had told me that there were only two brothers, no other siblings, and I knew that George was with me, so that doesn't leave much room for doubt.'

'No, I don't think that it does.' The sergeant seemed disappointed. At least a serious discrepancy would have made a starting point. 'When did you see him last? Alive,' he added.

It was Douglas's belief that questions should be answered literally. 'I saw him yesterday morning, but that was only through a window and he was fetching something from his van. Or maybe that was George – they were rather similar in appearance although their characters seemed very different. Apart from that possible glimpse I hadn't seen him for several days before that.'

'And Miss Jamieson?'

Tash stiffened as attention switched to her. She was shy but positive. 'I met him in the garden the day before yesterday. And it really was Stan, not George. There's a large greenhouse hidden from here behind the big clump of rhododendrons and he was coming back from that direction carrying a trug of early vegetables and a small fork. We stopped and spoke. We agreed that winter seemed to be over and we might get a decent summer for a change, if that's of any interest.'

'I see.' The sergeant looked from one to the other. 'And neither of you noticed anything out of the ordinary about him or his manner?'

'Nothing at all,' said Douglas.

Tash agreed and nodded. 'Nothing.'

'How about Mr George Eastwick?' the sergeant asked

suddenly. 'Was his manner and behaviour just what you would expect?'

The tense silence lasted for as long as it took a group of Tash's younger siblings to race across the grass below the window and vanish into the trees.

'I've been wondering about that,' Douglas said. 'I think I'd made up my mind to tell you although I'm sure you could see the point for yourself. It struck me at the time as strange that he should be so determined to have a witness along when he was going to look for his brother. It can't have been the first time that he'd searched for him but he's never needed company before.'

'From which you concluded . . .?'

'The possible inferences are obvious but I didn't draw any conclusions. That's your job. It just struck me as odd.'

'And you, Miss Jamieson?'

'I didn't want to be the first to tell you; but yes, it seemed strange to me.'

Sounds of a vehicle came up from the driveway below. The sergeant rose and looked down through the window. He spoke over his shoulder. 'Please say as little as possible outside this room. Your news flash, plus the information that there's no obvious cause of death, seems to say all that needs saying so please leave it at that. Your neighbours can be counted on to draw their own conclusions from our presence about the place. I'll be back, probably tomorrow.'

'What about the dog?' Douglas asked. 'Will George be staying there to look after her? Or will you take her away? Or what?'

The sergeant turned round to face the room. 'I was wondering about that,' he said. He had obviously forgotten altogether about Winnie. He paused at the door. 'The flat will be sealed up until the forensic investigators have finished with it. Mr George Eastwick will have to move out. Would anybody here be prepared to offer him a bed?'

'I think that's highly unlikely,' Douglas said. Frankness

seemed to be called for. 'It's not that people don't have the space. We just can't stand the man at any price. He seems to be in a state of permanent disgruntlement.'

'It's not just the loss of his brother, then?' The sergeant looked towards the heavens. 'Arrangements will be made,' he said. 'But I don't think that Mrs Laird will want a bulldog in the dog unit. Could I ask you to keep her for a day or two?'

'I can manage that,' Douglas said. 'Two dogs are not much more bother than one and she's a friendly old thing.'

The soundproofing of the building was good. When the door was closed, Douglas had to listen hard to be sure that the sergeant had gone downstairs and was not eavesdropping. 'The good sergeant might just as well have his thoughts written in magic marker in a balloon over his head.'

Tash nodded sombrely. 'You'd have to be dim not to suspect that Mr Eastwick knew that his brother was dead and wanted a witness to be with him when he found him. The person who finds a body is always a suspect, at least in the stories.'

Douglas was recovering from the shock of finding Stan's body. Treating the death as an episode in a detective story seemed to help. 'I think it's the same in real life. A killer won't fancy waiting for somebody else to make the discovery while wondering what they'll find that he hasn't thought of. He would have to fight against the temptation to return, as they say, to the scene of the crime to make certain. I expect that a higher percentage of killers than is statistically probable try to be present when the body's found, in order to offer innocent explanations for anomalies. But bodies must often be found by people who are quite innocent of any crime and Stan may have choked on a biscuit crumb, so I suggest that we don't jump to any conclusions. Stan may be found to have dropped dead of his own accord and George found him and preferred not to figure as the solo finder.'

'It's all very sad,' said Tash. 'Shall I go and put notes through letterboxes?'

TEN

I t was not to be expected that the other householders would accept the death of Stan Eastwick as a simple fact unworthy of comment. Uninformed discussion buzzed in the communal areas. Tash and Douglas were battered with a thousand questions but they were able to say with almost perfect truth that they knew no more than had been in the circulated note.

The activity of the half-dozen or so police officers who infested Stan's flat was evident, but to the interested observer, which comprised everyone whose age ran into double figures, it was the sort of activity to be expected when everybody knows that there is a problem but nobody is quite sure what it is. Searches were made for nothing in particular and endless statements were taken that seemed to be heading nowhere.

Just as vague and pointless was the gathering of occupiers on the evening of the following day. George Eastwick was not present and it was understood that, because the police still had desultory possession of the basement part of the property, he had returned temporarily to the flat that he still owned in Falkirk where the sale had not yet been completed. This was the one sale that had not been entrusted to Douglas and it gave him some quiet amusement to see the confusion that was causing delays.

There was still no news as to how and why Stan Eastwick had died, nor was it known whether he had ever made a will. The only decision possible was that meantime the upkeep of the gardens would have to be shared between the owners or entrusted to a contractor and the cost similarly shared. It was soon clear that the other occupiers shared

Douglas's pleasure in having access to a garden along with a rooted dislike of working in it. It was a time of year when gardens need attention. It was agreed that a man would be hired from the garden centre for two days a week, to work under Douglas's direction and the cost shared.

Almost exactly forty-eight hours after the discovery of the body, the suspense was relieved. A Detective Chief Inspector Laird arrived from Edinburgh. DCI *Alexander* Laird as he introduced himself, so Douglas surmised there was another DCI Laird somewhere in the Lothian and Borders Constabulary.

The surviving male occupiers had gone to their daily work and none of the women or children had known Stan Eastwick as more than a shadow sometimes seen preparing his flat or tidying the garden. Douglas was out, surveying a block of shops and flats in Morningside with Tash accompanying him to hold the tape and make notes. They returned to Underwood House to find that the chief inspector, lacking any other witnesses to question, was fuming at their absence and yet too busy studying the scene and finding fault with the earlier work to give them his immediate attention. Tash and Douglas had taken a snack lunch and then drafted an outline report on the property and were doing some calculations based on the survey measurements when Sergeant Dodson begged admission over the entry phone, was buzzed in but still knocked politely before entering.

'DCI Laird wants to see you shortly,' he said. 'No hurry,' he added as Douglas prepared to rise. 'He's still reading reports. He just wants you to stand by and not go out again. And between you and me you'd better watch what you say. Give him the facts and that's all. He's not in the best of moods. His top is ready to blow.'

'Thank you for the warning,' Douglas said.

'Who rattled his cage?' Tash asked. 'Was it you?'

'No, thank God! But that won't save me if I put a foot

wrong.' The sergeant seated himself. 'We'll wait. He will soon be heading in this direction. He was too fed up to eat any lunch so if you want to get into his good books make him a pot of tea and a sandwich.'

'I'll do it,' Tash said. She jumped up. 'But after warning us to be careful what we say the least you can do is to tell us what subjects to avoid. We won't let on that you told us.'

The sergeant thought about it and then nodded. 'I think you should avoid the subjects of promotion. And matrimony. I'll make myself scarce, for the moment,' DS Dodson said. He slipped outside.

'A proper respect for seniority, do you think?' Douglas said. 'Or does the sergeant have something on his conscience?'

'The former, I hope,' Tash said.

The entryphone announced that Chief Inspector Laird had arrived and was on the way upstairs. For Douglas, the penny suddenly dropped. So there had been two DCI Lairds. It came back to him that he had read in one of the local tabloids that the Lairds were a married couple – most unusual in the police and not often permitted unless each is extremely well thought of. The paper had reported, with cruel relish, that Mrs Laird had been promoted to equal rank with her husband. It had hinted that trouble might be expected in the marital nest. That had been some little time ago. There had been a photograph of Mrs Laird: beautiful and very well turned out, as indeed she should be with two good salaries in the family and, according to the press, an extremely well-heeled daddy. She had been born Honoria Potterton-Phipps, so that the nickname Honeypot had been inevitable. The sergeant's well intentioned but incautious remark now made sense. It did not require any great feat of deduction to realize that Mrs Laird had come to outrank her husband.

Detective Chief Inspector Alexander Laird turned out to

be a well built man of around forty with pale, gingery hair and an off-the-peg suit that fitted him adequately. If he had been in a bad mood he had risen above it, because his bland face showed little expression. His eyes flickered over the tray that Tash had provided, and when the four were seated around Douglas's desk he accepted tea and a sandwich with what was almost a cheerful smile. The sergeant had correctly guessed that Mr Laird would bear his apparent humiliation more easily away from the company of his colleagues.

'I had rather hoped to start with Professor Cullins,' he said.

'If there was a large, red, Japanese four-by-four at the door when you came in, he's back,' said Douglas. 'If not, not.'

'Ah. I rather wanted a little technical help and he does have a – um – partner who is a technician in biological sciences, so I'm told.'

'They usually travel together,' Tash explained.

While helping himself to another sandwich the DCI nodded. He had learned the habit of taking small bites so that he could take in food without suspending his enquiries. 'I'll come to the point. The post-mortem examination of Mr Eastwick's body will take some time. There's no obvious physical evidence. We'll have to wait for the results of analysis. All we know meantime is that there are very few signs of a cause of death. He seems to have died from some sort of suffocation but there are no signs of violence as would be the case with strangulation.'

Douglas at one time had done a great deal of commuting by train and had consumed innumerable murder stories to pass the journeys. In so doing, he had picked up some knowledge of forensic science. 'The hyoid bone was intact?' he asked before he could stop himself. 'Were there petechiae?'

'Yes.' The DCI looked at him in some surprise. 'You know about strangulation?'

'Only what I've read in murder mysteries. There was a time when I commuted by train for an hour each way. I read hundreds of them.' Douglas wondered whether to say something wise about Tardieu spots but decided that enough was enough.

DCI Laird looked at him hopefully. 'I didn't have the advantage of your upbringing and my medical colleagues enjoy mystifying me. Can you tell me what hypercapnia is?'

'I have heard the word,' Douglas said. He paused and thought back. 'It was in connection with an elderly uncle of mine whose heart was giving out. When he wasn't on oxygen he gasped for breath and he was said to be hypercapnic.'

'Thank you.' The DCI looked disappointed, but whether this was at the information or because he had finished the last sandwich Douglas was unsure. Tash was making short-hand symbols in her secretarial book.

Chief Inspector Laird asked her, 'Are you making notes?'

Tash put down her pen hurriedly. 'I didn't think you'd mind.'

For the first time a smile broke through the DCI's features. 'I don't mind. While my sergeant's otherwise engaged and he is monopolizing the wire recorder I have to make my own record, and I have a great dislike of trying to remember what everybody said almost as much as I hate making notes at the time and taking down my own words as I'm saying them. If you can make a record or even just a précis of our discussion I'll be in your debt.'

Returning his smile, Tash picked up her pen again.

'And there were no signs of his face having been covered?' Douglas asked helpfully.

'They'll be looking for signs now but I'm not very hopeful. Unless somebody's very sick or feeble or doped, signs of violence are usually very evident. My – um – wife had just such a case recently.' The DCI took a second to remove the faintly pained expression that had accompanied

the word 'wife'. 'A preliminary comment by the pathologist suggests that the carbon dioxide level in his blood was
slightly raised. Of course, the body was found in a very
confined space but not nearly small enough for his own
breathing to account for it and there were no signs that he
had been indulging in much physical activity.'

'There are drugs that paralyse the breathing,' Douglas
said.

The DCI seemed to be relaxing. It would be unusual for
an officer to discuss technical details of a case with a lay
witness, but if he was sensitive about his wife's promotion
he might well be in need of another knowledgeable person
off whom to bounce ideas. 'So the pathologist said. No
doubt he's testing for them while we speak, but that can
be a lengthy process. So we'll find out all we can by less
technical means. I have the general background – a large
old house subdivided into luxury apartments, with what
may ultimately turn into a granny flat in the semi-basement
being sold to the deceased against an undertaking to main-
tain the garden. I fear that you may have made a bad
bargain there.'

'So do I,' Douglas said. 'The only redeeming feature is
that it gave all the occupiers a motive to keep him alive,
which may simplify your enquiries a little.'

'Possibly true,' said the DCI. 'So we'll just have to hope
that no motive for his death, even stronger than any desire to
protect your investment, raises its head.'

Douglas tried to smile but the DCI did not seem to have
been joking. 'We don't know if he made a will,' Douglas
said, 'nor what it says if he did; but I suppose it's too
much to hope that he left his apartment to a keen gardener
on condition that he takes over responsibility for the
gardens.'

The chief inspector chuckled without showing a sign of
genuine amusement. 'You should be so lucky,' he said.
'What can you tell me about the deceased?'

'Not a lot.' When he came to think about it, Douglas was surprised to realize how little he had known about the late Stan Eastwick. 'He was introduced by the professor, who knew that Stan had been second in command of gardening at the university. From my own university days, I know that that's quite a responsible job. Universities have acres of gardens and greenhouses and some of those are used for research or teaching projects in biological sciences. Three or four of us interviewed him and he satisfied us that he knew his stuff and wanted to make use of it in his retirement. I checked to make sure that he owned his own flat and so could afford our price for this one, and that he was not averse to physical work. Beyond that point he seemed to be inoffensive. He liked dogs,' Douglas added, 'and dogs liked him.'

The chief inspector brightened. Rowan had already settled against his leg and was snuffling with pleasure at having his ears pulled. 'That's your criterion, is it?'

Douglas laughed. 'Not the only one. Dogs can take to a person who smells of dog biscuits or other dogs. But sometimes their first impression is more reliable than mine. What else can I tell you? He was a very handy person – not just in the garden, although he could arrange picked flowers to look better and last longer than anyone else could. But if anyone wanted his help with anything electrical or mechanical he could usually manage it. He'll be missed.'

'By you, perhaps, but not by Miss Jamieson. She looks disapproving whenever his name's mentioned.'

As far as Douglas was aware the DCI had hardly ever looked directly at Tash. Either he could be observant out of the corner of his eye or he had brought telepathy to a fine art.

'He was a bum-pincher,' Tash said defensively.

Now that the building was more or less finished and paid for, Douglas was only an owner-occupier among others, but he still felt a responsibility. 'Why didn't you say something?' he asked. 'One of us could at least have given him a good talking-to.'

Tash was turning pink. She paused to order her thoughts. 'It wasn't serious enough for that. It was never anywhere you might call intimate. Just fleshy, if you see what I mean.'

Douglas was distracted for a moment by the thought that he would have loved to see what she meant. 'Did you catch him looking at you?'

'Yes. But girls rather expect that. Most of us begin to wonder what's wrong if men's eyes don't follow us.'

While Tash was in this mood of unusual outspokenness, Douglas would have been interested to pursue the subject; but this was not the occasion. The chief inspector seemed to be of a like mind. 'But he was on good terms with the residents?'

'I never heard of any quarrels,' Douglas said. 'He was generally liked.'

Tash shrugged her answer.

'Did he have any special areas of interest outside horticulture?'

Douglas decided that he could safely leave rumours of an amorous past to be mentioned by others. 'Not that I know of,' he said.

'Very well. Let's move on. George Eastwick. Tell me about him.'

'A surly and evil-tempered man. If I had to sum him up in a single word, I think it would be "malevolent". He rubbed along with his brother for most of the time, but even those two could snap at each other. Just let anyone else rub George up the wrong way and he can turn ugly. Of course, he had nothing to lose. The worst we could have done in return would have been to forbid him the place, which would only have cost Stan the help he was getting. Where we go from here, God alone knows! We'll just have to wait until Stan's will has been read, if he ever made one.'

'What's George's job, trad
'I never heard him talk
and pieces of convers
gamekeeper or a ge
estate.'

DCI Laird pondered qu.
about the adult residents he.

'Very well,' Douglas said. '

'I'll hear about you from the c
clear vision of himself, and if he h
wraps. Give me your origin and CV h
tell me about the professor.'

Tash seemed to be listening intently w
summary of his upbringing in Perth, the move
to suit his father's work in the civil service and
duction into surveying by an uncle. Ah well. Curic
a woman's perquisite.

ELEVEN

'I know about one per cent of damn all about the professor,' Douglas said. 'Mrs Jamieson introduced him, so perhaps she can wise you up. But perhaps not. I'm a bit nervous of homosexuals, for no good reason that I can think of, so I've been steering clear of him and his partner. I can only say that he's been well behaved. He sometimes flavours his speech with minor swear words, but he explains that that's to help the scansion. The rhythm of the sentence, you understand? I don't think that anyone but himself would notice the difference. Apart from that, he and his partner are polite and friendly to everyone but they don't go out of their way to be sociable. Mostly they keep themselves to themselves. They often go out in the evening but they never bring anybody back here.'

The chief inspector shifted his eyes to Tash. She seemed to feel their arrival because she looked up from her shorthand book.

'All I could add,' she said slowly, 'is that the professor seems to like young people. He always stops for a chat with any of the children and he bought me chocolates for Christmas, pushing them at me gruffly as though he was ashamed of it.' She lowered her eyes to the laptop screen before returning them to her very neat shorthand.

'Thank you. And now I'll ask you not to interrupt while Mr Young tells me about your mother and Mrs McLeish. That's if Mr Young doesn't mind talking openly in front of you.'

Tash mimed zipping up her lips.

'I don't have a problem. To me, they're just two pleasant and very well preserved ladies,' Douglas said. 'They get on well together, which is a blessing. Tash's mum is the more forceful and outspoken one while Mrs McLeish is the retiring sort. They go off to the kirk together on Sundays – not, I think, because they're seriously religious but because it's what one does. They do most of the cooking although they keep off the fatty foods themselves; they care about their figures. They represent the backbone of society, two ladies who don't care about much beyond home and children, but when confronted with a problem come down on the side of common sense. Tash's father was home on leave for a few weeks in . . . December, was it?'

'January,' Tash said.

'January sounds right. I saw very little of him because he spent the whole time painting and papering. Betty McLeish's husband is an old friend of mine. He owns and runs his garage, service and filling station and has an agency for new cars, but he's surrounded himself with competent staff so he's never too busy to take a little time off. He shuts everything down on Sundays except for a small team of part-timers manning the pumps. He keeps the day for himself. He has a temper but he's learned to control it – he'd have to, running a business with a substantial turnover.'

'And neither of you ever overheard a quarrel between the deceased and any of the residents, adult or children?'

Tash shook her head.

Douglas said, 'Stan didn't seem to be the quarrelsome sort. Between the gardens and his flat he was too busy to go out much and I don't remember him ever having visitors. Whenever I had to call on him in connection with the flat he'd invite me in for a glass of his home brew. If George offers you a glass, be very wary. That stuff could blow your head off.'

'I'll remember.' The detective chief inspector scowled at the window for some seconds. 'Tell me, which of the residents here could you imagine getting angry enough or ruthless enough to kill somebody?'

'Nobody,' Tash said quickly.

'Almost anybody,' Douglas said an instant later. 'There are very few people in the world who couldn't be provoked into lashing out.'

Tash looked at Douglas in surprise. This cynical side to his character was new to her.

The DCI was nodding slowly. Evidently his experience was in accord with Douglas's. 'But this wasn't a case of lashing out,' he said at last, 'this was something thought out, planned and carried through. Well, there will be more such questions, but I don't know yet what they are. What can you tell me about carbon dioxide?'

Douglas decided that the officer was interested in how much they would admit to knowing rather than seeking enlightenment on the subject itself. The answer was the same anyway. 'Very little,' he said. 'It isn't a poison like monoxide, it suffocates by replacing oxygen. We breathe it out all the time and plants breathe it in. That's about the lot.'

'A lot of it goes into fizzy drinks,' Tash said. 'It's produced naturally in huge quantities. It's used in fire-fighting and refrigeration. They use it for artificial smoke or fog in the theatre. Sometimes it's used as the inert gas in welding processes and also for hardening the casting moulds for metals.' She was hiding a trace of a complacent smile.

Such a rush of erudition was unprecedented. There was a stunned silence. The detective chief inspector broke it with an effort. 'How do you know all this?'

She tapped the laptop. 'I've just Googled it. Sometimes carbon dioxide is used in greenhouses because carbon dioxide from the air is where plants get most of the carbon for growing, not from fertilizers in the ground. The oxygen part gets returned to the atmosphere. But that particular process is reversed slightly at night, which is why they take flowers out of a sickroom at night.'

The detective chief inspector made an irritated sound. 'And the deceased was a gardener! It's used as the inert gas in welding and Mr McLeish has a garage and workshop. And I suppose the university uses it?'

'I would think so,' Douglas said. 'They have an anechoic chamber for noise experiments and anechoic chambers are lined with foam plastic which is very flammable. I would expect there to be a system for flooding the chamber with carbon dioxide whenever the smoke detectors are triggered. I did some work for the other university,' he explained. 'It must also be used a lot in both teaching and research, but you'd better ask the professor about that. Or Mr Campion, his technician friend.'

'I see. And does anybody here go in for amateur theatricals?'

'I'll save Tash the distress of having to be a telltale,' said Douglas. 'The two ladies do. I suspect that that's a major factor in their care for their figures. Their club is putting on *Oklahoma* in the autumn, I believe.'

The detective chief inspector sat back and closed his eyes for a minute. Douglas could almost believe that he was blinking back a tear. 'That's great!' he said. 'Oh, that's just dandy! To look at it from the other end, is there anybody around here who couldn't beg, borrow or steal a cylinder of carbon dioxide?'

'If you're going to start from the other end,' Douglas said, 'you'd better get on to the suppliers and find out who they've supplied it to.'

That was too much. 'Thank you for your helpful suggestion,' said DCI Laird through gritted teeth. 'I would never have thought of that for myself,' He got to his feet and stalked out of the room.

'Ouch!' Douglas said. 'I should have remembered how insulting it is to be told to do what you were going to do anyway. You'd better type up your notes and we'll give them to him quickly as a peace offering.'

'All of them?'

'Stop after the mention of *Oklahoma!*'

Tash looked at her notes. 'I see what you mean.'

TWELVE

Douglas's major client had a job for him. It had lain fallow for months and then, when the client had at last made up its many minds, the job had been deemed urgent. He and Natasha took an early breakfast and escaped the clutches of their curious neighbours only to be bearded at the car door by a newspaper reporter. The media, it seemed, knew only that a man had been found dead. Under pressure by a practised interrogator to reveal who had found the body, Douglas had at length admitted that he had been present when the body was found.

'But I did not see anything to explain the death,' he said with truthfulness, 'so bugger off. And you can quote me on that.'

'That goes for me too,' said Tash; but she glanced at herself in the car's wing mirror before she allowed the reporter to photograph her. The photograph, delicately airbrushed, eventually appeared along with a hint that it had been Tash who found the body. It was then that she learned that, in the view of the media, any dramatic event or provocative opinion is attributed to the prettiest girl in sight at the time.

Douglas and Tash spent the day carrying out a survey of a rambling industrial building that was now vacated and derelict. They had developed a teamwork aimed at minimizing their time spent working and maximizing their precious leisure time. Provided that Douglas drove gently and gave warning of any bumps ahead, Tash could take dictation direct onto the laptop in the moving car. Douglas thought freely while driving and while his recollection of the building was fresh. The buildings that they had been surveying could be converted into dwellings as the client hoped, but Douglas's report pointed out that the neighbourhood had become almost a slum and that more than thirty old houses would have to be updated or demolished to restore housing values in the area. It might be essential to enlarge the project. The capital requirement would be greater but so also would be the profitability. He could produce or obtain more accurate figures if instructed.

That conclusion had not taken long to reach. Expecting to run late, Douglas had said that they would not be back in time for an evening meal so they stopped at the Lothian Arms, a good quality pub not far from Underwood House, for a bar supper. The pub's decoration was inoffensive and there was no jukebox.

Over the scampi and chips he asked her, 'Do you have any ideas about what might have happened to Stan?'

Tash considered the question. 'From what the police are asking, they still haven't found a cause of death that they can be sure of. I think he just plain died.'

The licensee was a huge man, built to a large scale and then enlarged further by obesity. His name was Swanson and Douglas had surveyed and valued the pub on behalf of the brewery owners.

After greeting Douglas and his assistant, Swanson came and leaned over their table. 'So you've lost one of your residents?'

'That's so.'

'The fat little bugger? Stan something?'

'Eastwick,' Douglas said. 'Yes. Did he come in here?'

'From time to time. Not very often. Just as well. We can do without his sort in here.'

Douglas was surprised. Stan Eastwick had always seemed friendly and without vice or malice. 'He didn't make trouble, did he?'

Swanson sank his bulk into a chair that creaked in protest.

'Not exactly, no. But it was only a matter of time, the way he looked.'

Tash seemed to understand but this seemed very strange to Douglas. Stan Eastwick's appearance had never seemed out of the ordinary. 'Looked?'

'At women,' Swanson said impatiently. 'As if he could see through their clothes. X-ray vision or something. My wife was complaining.'

Mrs Swanson was a looker and she knew it; tall, brassy blonde, with long and shapely legs, she carried her large bust proudly before her. Her face, though, come to think of it, Douglas could not remember her face, if he had ever seen it. This was definitely a subject to be avoided.

'And his brother?' Douglas asked. 'Did he seem to have X-ray vision too?'

Swanson considered his reply. 'Not that I noticed,' he said at last. 'He's more like one who's afraid of women. Looked away and cut it short if the wife spoke to him. Know what I mean?'

'Where is Mrs Swanson today?' Tash asked idly. 'Gone out with the girls?'

'She's down in the cellar putting on a fresh carbon dioxide cylinder. I'd better go and see what's keeping her.' He rose and lumbered away.

Douglas decided not to comment on the mention of gas cylinders. 'I don't think anybody ever just dies,' he said. 'There has to be a reason. Nothing ever happens without a reason.'

'Are you sure of that?'

'Not a damn bit,' he admitted. 'That's the sort of thinking that leads to the assumption of the existence of an all-seeing and all-deciding God.'

They spent the rest of the meal arguing amicably over religion. It was a subject about which disagreement was all too easy so Douglas usually avoided it, but on this occasion he found that he and Tash had identically agnostic views.

As they got into the car Tash said, 'So they use carbon dioxide to push the beer up to the pumps. And to keep it from going flat. I think Mr Swanson did it. I think he set a trap for George Eastwick but his brother walked into it.' Douglas had to look at her twice to make sure that she was joking.

When they reached home, Douglas was pleased to see that there were no reporters besieging the front door. Police vehicles, he discovered, were discreetly parked at the back door and had not yet been discovered by the media.

Tash went to write up the report from their morning's meeting into Douglas's distinctive format and onto email.

Douglas was using the original drawing room as his office. He never entertained more than a very few people at a time so that what had been a small dressing room was quite large enough for his sitting room. He had retained it for that purpose and was preparing to put his feet up when an uncharacteristically polite tapping at the door announced the arrival of George Eastwick.

'Can I have a word?' he asked.

Douglas was tired and he had no great liking for George but he preferred not to get on bad terms with one who might well become a neighbour. There was nothing on the television that anybody with two brain cells could want to watch. Even the Discovery channel could only reveal an obsession with the sexual customs of early man. He was relieved to see that Tash's siblings were playing Vulcans and Borgs among the trees. He found that he had already read his library book. He could hardly grudge George a word, especially after so polite an approach. He bit back the first word to spring to his mind and invited George to come in and sit.

George seemed unimpressed with the room. 'Why d'you squeeze yourself into this pokey wee hole?' he demanded. 'You've a grand room across the hall and you only use it as an office.'

Douglas felt the need to explain – to himself as much as to George. 'I need an impressive office. In here, I'm as often just myself or with one or two friends. If I ever get a live-in girlfriend again I might swap them over, if that's what she wants. I'll hope to hold meetings in my office when business builds up.' In his secret mind, Douglas was determined that any lady planning to move in with him would be the sort who enjoyed intimate comfort above display. The other kind would be strictly a one-nighter. 'Anyway, it costs less to light and heat.'

George nodded. That argument he could understand. 'I wanted to ask you . . . to ask you . . .'

'Yes?'

'What did you tell yon chief inspector about me?'

Douglas had no wish to start a list of his enemies with George's name but he had no objection to giving him a heavily edited version of what he had said to DCI Laird. He decided that he might as well pick up some information in exchange. 'I don't remember saying much about you. He wanted a summary of everybody in the house. Of course, I had to tell him about how we came to find your brother. When do they say that Stan died?'

'They've not said. But we found him on Wednesday and they were asking me what I was doing all day on Monday. I said I went back to Falkirk to see was there any mail or messages for me and to renew my prescriptions. If they ask you, you'll mind that my van was away all day. What did you say about why you came with me?'

'Just that you'd asked me to come along,' Douglas said. Tash had finished sending the email and arrived in the doorway. Douglas patted the chair next to his. 'What else did they ask you?'

'Och, a' damn thing. Like how did I get on wi' Stan.'

Douglas noticed that while Tash was in the room George turned his shoulder towards her and lowered his voice slightly. 'I told them we was good friends and if I was

going to kill one of us it would've been me. No need to
look so shocked. In the Guid Book it says that the years
of our lives are three score and ten. It says we may linger
on to fourscore, but I've gone past that.'

Douglas was genuinely surprised. 'You don't look it.'

George frowned but looked modest. 'It's true a' the same.
Stan was fifteen years my junior, though you wouldn't have
known it from the way he ordered me around. And when
you get this old all your bits wear out together. They work
a' right but they're sair. It's easier to count the parts that
don't trouble you than the ones that do. Life's no' so
precious as it was. They kept asking me what I knew about
monoxide and did Stan keep any.'

The sudden return to the earlier subject had Douglas
blinking. 'You mean dioxide, don't you? Carbon dioxide?'

George shrugged irritably. 'Carbon something anyway.
There's a cylinder of something of the sort in the big
greenhouse but I don't know what Stan had it for. He said
something once about doing some tests for somebody in
the botany department.'

Douglas found that his memory was coming alive. There
had been something on Discovery that Tash had repeated,
'Plants take up very little food for growth through their
roots. They need carbon to make material for growth but
they get most of that from the carbon dioxide in the air.'

'That'll be it, then. But that cylinder hasn't been touched
for a while. There's dust and cobwebs a' over it.' George
was uncomfortable. The little, involuntary movements that
people make while speaking had ceased.

Douglas caught Tash's eye. They were developing an
understanding which often made spoken words unneces-
sary, minute changes in body language being sufficient.
This had proved valuable when confronting a householder
who was prepared to swear that there had never been rot
in the house while Douglas's nose was insisting that there
was dry rot in the area of the staircase. He had kept the

householder talking while Tash had slipped back to examine the understairs space away from which they had been firmly shepherded. Sure enough, the strands of *merulius lachrymans* were unmistakeable.

Tash left the room.

'Do you know whether Stan ever made a will?'

George's eyes narrowed as if to prevent the escape of his anger. 'What's it to you if he did?'

Douglas hid a sigh. He had no alternative to showing his best card. 'We let Stan have the flat at a thief's bargain price on condition that he looked after the gardens for us.'

'Well, you needn't look at me. Stan bought it, free and clear, and he said he wouldn't make a will because what he had would come to me anyway. And I'm not digging gardens at my age. Get somebody in to see to't and I'll pay my whack. But nothing fancy, mind. There's a dozen people living here and I'm only one, so I'll pay a twelfth.'

Douglas knew only too well that while the courts are often happy to order and enforce the paying over of money they have great difficulty enforcing a positive action. 'It was a debt of honour,' he said, 'and Stan would have honoured the bargain.' He had never counted heads but he wondered if George had had to include Mrs Jamieson's foetus to make the number up to a dozen.

'I wasn't party to the bargain,' George said. The sneer in his voice was reflected in his eyes. 'And I'm damned if I'll honour it. Emdy wants my honour they can have it, gift-wrapped. You needn't look at me all superior; you'll get your comeuppance. You should have heard some of the questions they were asking about you.'

'Like what?' Douglas knew that he was innocent. Nevertheless, he felt the beginning of an internal cringe at the thought of suggestions being made to his neighbours concerning his integrity.

'I'm not telling you like what. You can wait and find out the hard way.' George got up and headed for the door.

Douglas let him go. Tash had had time to get to the greenhouse. She returned after an interval suggesting that she had waited out of sight rather than risk meeting George on the stairs.

'One cylinder,' she said, settling herself in her chair again, 'clean and shining like new.'

'You wouldn't expect it to be clean and shining after standing around in a greenhouse. You'd expect dust and cobwebs, just as George described it. And I can't imagine Stan going to the trouble of washing it or even wiping it down.'

Tash looked at him with her eyes very wide. 'You think somebody used it and then cleaned it off in case of finger-prints or something?'

'That,' Douglas said, 'or that somebody wanted to incriminate George.'

THIRTEEN

'It will soon be time,' Tash said, 'that I went to my lonely little bed. My mother will be thinking that we're up to all sorts of shenanigans.'

'We haven't had dinner yet.'

'I meant dinner.' She paused, expectantly.

There had been plenty in her brief statement to set Douglas's mind working and his hormones coursing round his veins. Surely it could not have been a Freudian slip. Instead, he was reminded to take a brown envelope out of his pocket and hand it over. 'I was almost forgetting to pay you.'

'Thank you.' Tash opened the envelope, peeped inside and riffled the edges of the notes with her thumb. She sucked in breath through her teeth. 'This is much more than you've been paying me up until now.'

'You're becoming much more valuable.' Douglas had hesitated over raising the subject and had decided on an oblique approach via what amounted almost to a *fait accompli*. 'And if you want to join me full-time, there could be a job for you. My assistant as well as my secretary-typist-telephonist cum filing clerkess. You could study part-time for your qualification. That's if the subject interests you.'

'Oh, it does,' she said. She flushed – with pleasure he hoped and believed. 'People are interesting but they're not always logical. Sometimes they're impossible to explain. In buildings, as you said, nothing happens without a reason. There are detective stories hidden everywhere. Every little bit of them tells you something about the people who went before. And facts are facts when you can reach them, not like most subjects where no two people agree about anything.'

She fell silent. Douglas waited, admiring the soft curve of her cheek. 'It's a wonderful offer,' she said at last. 'It solves about ten thousand problems for me, all at the same time. Well, two or three.'

Douglas appreciated the gesture towards precision.

She paused again. She was turning pink and he noticed that she was twisting her hands together so tightly that her fingers were white. She was infinitely desirable and equally out of bounds. 'My first impulse is to take you up on it quickly before you can change your mind.' She was speaking rapidly, almost gabbling. 'But there's one subject that we should get out of the way first. You see, I'm a virgin.'

This came as a surprise – not the revelation but the mention of it. He tried to keep any amusement out of his voice. 'I would have supposed so,' he said. 'It's not a requirement for the job and if you come to work for me I wouldn't try to change that. Your private life would be your own.'

Her colour went from rose pink to dusky scarlet. 'No, no,' she said. 'That's not what I meant at all. Don't hurry me, just let me explain slowly and calmly, if I can.' She took several deep breaths. 'It's this way. I've had boys chasing after me and wanting you-know-what, and I could have, but something held me back. Not just fear of getting it all wrong. And not just the fact that there wasn't one of them that I could even imagine myself in love with. I've listened to other girls, ones who've been doing it, and I'm confused. There are some who say that it's not all it's cracked up to be, nothing special at all, and others say that it's the greatest feeling in the world. And they say that you don't enjoy the first time because it hurts. And nobody can explain how it's supposed to feel. Mum explained how it all works but she could only talk about love in the abstract and contraception and about being swept off your feet and I can imagine all that stuff. Novels are full of it.'

'Whereas you want to know what lust and orgasm feel like?'

She relaxed visibly and her colour began to subside. 'That's it exactly. Then I can make up my own mind about these things. And I thought that you're about the nicest man I know and, if you don't mind my saying so, you're an attractive man in the prime of life. You'd know how it should really be and I know that you're not the sort who would talk about it afterwards. And I also know that you've had lady friends but you don't seem to be attached at the moment.'

Douglas felt his heart lift. He desired Tash but he had set his mind against making a pass at one so young and innocent; yet here she was, making a delightfully naïve pass at him. He was sure that if they tiptoed around the subject for much longer he would burst – probably with laughter. Somebody would have to drag the subject into the open by the scruff of its neck.

'You want me to give you your first experience?' he said, hardly believing his ears.

Her gasp was definitely one of relief. 'Once again, yes, that's it. That's if you don't mind,' she added anxiously.

Douglas struggled to hide all expression. 'Of course I wouldn't mind. How could I possibly? You're hugely attractive. Not many men could look at you and not want you. It's been my favourite daydream. It would be a delightful privilege. But you do realize that there may be emotional consequences. I'm not saying that such consequences are bad. They may be great. But they're there.'

'You mean like falling in love? I wouldn't want to be in a position to hurt your feelings. But I don't think we should talk about love. I'm too young for that. So no flowers, please or . . . or chocolates, or anything like that.'

'Not even a diamond or two?'

'Now you're just being silly.'

Douglas felt that they had gone quite far enough along that road. He had fulfilled his obligations. 'When did you have in mind?'

Tash suddenly looked ten years younger. She fingered the hem of her skirt. 'How about now? It needn't take long, need it?'

'With your mother liable to come looking for you at any moment? And here comes the most important part of the lesson. It *should* take a long time. Those girls who told you that it was nothing special, they had been with the wrong sort of boy, the kind who takes his pleasure quickly and then hurries away, leaving the girl unsatisfied. The important thing, the most vital thing, is to wait until she's . . .' He ground to a halt, uncertain of how to explain without shocking her out of her mind.

'It's all right,' she said hastily. 'I think I know what you mean. Until she's ready.'

'Yes. So on some occasion when we can be secure against interruption for not less than an hour, minimum, preferably all evening or even all night . . .'

She produced her most shining smile. Now she was less embarrassed than he was. 'It will be something special to look forward to,' she said.

'It certainly will. We'd have to have an agreement that if we don't suit each other that way – it does sometimes happen – we'll just forget about it, no hard feelings on either side and go on just as we are now.'

'Yes! My mum was talking about going to spend a few days with my aunt in North Berwick, but if I was in a proper job . . .'

'She'd have to leave you here.'

'Yes.' She reached out a hand towards him. He was unsure what she expected him to do with it but he realized that they had not even touched fingers. No physical contact at all. He took her hand as if to shake it and she came to him as though pulled. He was determined not to kiss her so soon but he had no alternative.

The first touch of lips was nothing special. He had kissed many women and this was just one more. But then it became very special. It was not just that she had opened her very soft lips. It was more that she *meant* it. Just by touch she was sending messages.

He was still digesting the thought while enjoying the kiss when the latch clicked. They jumped apart. It was not Tash's mother but the youngest of Tash's siblings, Ella, who was sometimes sent to let Tash know that a meal or a visitor was waiting.

At four, Ella's vocabulary was still limited. 'Iggley biggley bopchick,' she said. It had become a favourite expression of hers. Nobody knew where it came from or what it was supposed to mean. They had decided that it probably resembled the sound of some phrase heard on television but not understood and that she guessed, from the audience reaction, that it had some significance. 'Come,' she added, clearly.

'We're coming,' Tash said huskily. The look she exchanged with Douglas said clearly, *Did she see us?* Ella's voice from the landing gave her the answer. 'Kissy-kissy.'

As she followed her little sister down the stairs Tash said loudly, 'I already gave you your kissy-kissy.' She sounded quite convincing. Ella was startled into silence. It was quick thinking.

Douglas was left to his thoughts. As she said, it would be something to look forward to – if she went through with it. It was the sort of promise that girls made and then got cold feet, or had never intended to keep anyway. Perhaps he had imagined the whole conversation. That the exquisite, adorable Tash should offer herself was the subject for a male fantasy. Time would tell.

FOURTEEN

Douglas was becoming restive. All that he wanted out of life was enough success in his chosen profession to let him live in reasonable comfort and without any doubts about his future security and some leisure time to pursue his other interests. Some female companionship would be a bonus.

This ideal state had seemed to be within his grasp, all but the female companionship, until the finding of Stan's body. Now, with policemen appearing and vanishing like pantomime fairies and unanswerable questions hanging in the wind, he was unsettled. Whenever he got his teeth into the next task it seemed that some quirk of the mystery would assume great importance, at least in the minds of the police, and he would be forced to choose between accepting the distractions from his life and work while he explained for the fourth or fifth time what he had thought was obvious to every visitor, as against telling the police to go and play in the pretty traffic. But the police have enviable facilities for letting the driver or homeowner or professional man know that they are less than happy, so offending them had to remain as a last resort.

To gain himself a little of the peace and quiet that he craved, Douglas went out for a walk. The day was Sunday. The law about Sunday shooting is confused but local prejudice is not, so he left his gun behind and carried a walking stick instead, to Rowan's disgust.

His muscles had become unused to the exercise but it felt good to stretch them again. They tired more quickly than they used to. He followed his favourite track up the hill, enjoying the sights and sounds and smells of the countryside while Rowan ranged to and fro, hoping to put up a pheasant but settling for the occasional rabbit. At the top of the hill Douglas was glad to take a seat on top of a dry stone wall, on a flat stone that he had used many times for the purpose. It was comfortable and warmed by the sun.

He was sitting upright but close to dozing off when a man's voice said, 'Mr Young?'

Before even opening his eyes he made up his mind that if this were another policeman there would be a short and blunt exchange of words, but when he opened his eyes the man was quite unpolicemanlike, being short, thickset, more than his own age and nervously pacific. He was dressed in rough tweeds. He came forward with his hand outstretched. 'I'm Norman Eastwick.'

Douglas had been aware of a faint sensation of *déjà vu*. This was now explained. 'I take it that you're the son of one of the Eastwick brothers.'

'I'm George's son. I . . . my parents never married although they lived together for some time, but I took his name for my mum's sake. I came through to see if he was all right, my uncle being dead and all like that. There was only one lady to be seen at the house and she said that you'd gone for a walk in this direction. So I followed you up.' His skin, Douglas noticed, was tanned as if from an outdoor life. His accent was faint and local.

'Why me in particular?' Douglas asked. 'Would she not have done? Allowed you to wait for your father to come home?'

'I didn't like to ask her – she seemed a bit of a hard nut.' (Mrs Jamieson, then, Douglas decided.) 'And from what I'd heard from my dad, you're the leader around here.'

Douglas was only slightly flattered. It was not a group in which it was difficult to be the leader. He got to his feet. 'I was going to head for home. Come along and you can wait for your father in my place.'

'That's good of you.'

They set off down the hill. Underwood House could be seen peeping through the treetops in the distance.

'I think you can take it that your father is quite all right,' said Douglas. 'He's staying in his brother's flat and gives the impression that he rather expects to inherit it. Maybe it will come to you eventually?'

'I hope so. It looks and sounds attractive.'

Douglas decided to fish a little. 'Stan got a favourable price on the condition that he would keep the gardens in order.'

'You won't get Dad to work in a garden. I'd take it on like a shot, I love gardening and Uncle Stan taught me a lot. Well, I'm glad to know that Dad's all right. But I think I'll wait and see him all the same. Set my mind at rest. What . . . what can you tell me about what happened to my uncle?'

'Nobody knows for sure.' Briefly, Douglas explained the terms of Stan's purchase of the basement flat, the discovery of his body and the general uncertainty as to what had caused his death.

'I see,' Norman Eastwick said. 'Thank you. I'd better go and speak to the police if you'll tell me who to contact. What you've told me makes me rather glad that I was abroad just then. I had a bit of holiday to come and I went on my motorbike and got pinched for speeding in France.'

'The French aren't so very disapproving of speed. You must have been going at some lick.'

'A hundred and thirty,' Norman said proudly. 'Miles an hour, not kilometres.'

They walked on in respectful silence. Underwood House vanished behind the trees. 'What do you do for a living?' Douglas enquired.

'I'm the keeper on a small estate the other side of Edinburgh.'

Douglas pricked up his ears at the mention of that

profession. He was tempted to raise the practicability of
turning out a few pheasants in the Underwood House
gardens with the intention of pursuing them on the
adjoining farmland, but he put the subject aside for later
discussion. 'How old were you when your parents separated?' he asked. He quickly added, 'Forgive my nosiness
but I never knew that there was any family . . .'

'That's all right. My mother took me away when I was
almost too young to remember. But then she died and
George, being my father, took over. They were good to
me, the two of them, my father and Uncle Stan. I only
moved out when I wanted to marry, about five years ago.
Uncle Stan had left by then to buy a flat nearer to his work.
I have a wife now and a young son.'

The conversation rambled. Norman expressed his satisfaction with his present life and prospects. They came
down to the fringe of the Underwood House policies. The
late Stan Eastwick had used his chainsaw to sculpt a bench
complete with seatback out of a fallen tree trunk where
the sitter could enjoy a view of the gardens and the house
and they took a seat.

'It's a handsome old place,' Norman said.

Douglas agreed but this was not the time for discussion
of the merits of Underwood House. 'George was helping
Stan with the finishings to his flat in the semi-basement,
but there was occasional friction. Did the two of them
always get on well together?'

'I think they tried hard not to quarrel in front of me.
Dad had a temper, there's no doubt about that. I suppose
he still has it. But it was always kept just under control.'

'Do you think that your presence was why he kept it
like that?'

Norman considered the question carefully. 'You could
be right. I never thought of it that way. But they did argue
sometimes and when they did it was usually a jealousy
thing – a squabble, not a blazing row.' He paused and

blinked at Douglas. 'I shouldn't be talking about them like this to a stranger but I suppose the police will want to know all about it and then it'll become public knowledge. They had something in common, an interest or a hobby or some such thing. That seemed to hold them together and if they quarrelled it was about that. But I've no idea what it was and I must admit that I'm as curious as anybody. They were much too secretive about it. They always made out that I was too young to understand – and that seemed to keep me from asking more questions. But I do still wonder what it is. You'd have to ask Dad, or the police will.'

Douglas was trying to think of an oblique way of fishing for more details when George's van (as it had become) came to the back of the house and stopped at the door of the basement flat. Once George had dismounted, his son, recognizing him even at a distance, shook hands with Douglas and hurried across the grass to intercept his father. Douglas sighed. If only Norman had been Stan's son instead of George's, he would have inherited the flat and have been a much better neighbour than George.

On the drive before the front door there stood a very handsome Japanese motorbike, sparkling chromium and polished stainless steel surrounding an engine that would have done many a small car proud. Douglas sighed again. If he had not settled into quite so respectable a lifestyle, he too might have worn black leather and blasted around sitting on several litres of raw power.

FIFTEEN

George was understood to be staying in his own flat in Falkirk while the police had possession of Stan's semi-basement flat in Underwood House. Occasionally he could be seen visiting the basement flat. He seemed to have reached an informal compromise – he would come and 'help the police with their inquiries' in exchange for being allowed to give some attention to preparations for the fitting-out of the kitchenette. Empty cartons from flat-pack kitchen units were piling up around the door.

A week after Norman's visit, Douglas's spirits fell when there was a knock on his inside door and he found George on the threshold. Apparently George was only a messenger on this occasion, but he never brought good news.

'There's somebody wants to see you. Something about Stan.'

This was Douglas's quiet Sunday and he did not want to waste it on worrying about the late Stan. He had been contentedly surfing the Internet and thinking about Tash. 'Tell him to –' there was a pause while Douglas moderated his language '– log off. Unless he wants property surveyed, that is.'

'He's from the university and he seems to be in a bit of a tizzy. You'd better see him.'

'If it's to do with Stan, you should see him. Stan was your brother.'

'I said that. He wants to see you.'

'Oh, all right,' Douglas said peevishly. The weather outside was foul, cold rain borne on a lashing wind, but he had been engrossed. 'I thought you'd gone home,' he said to George.

'Had to get out, the buyers wanted in and the police had finished here. This will be home as soon as they let me stay. I'll fetch your guest up.'

Douglas had just enough time to skip to the end of what he was reading and shut down the computer before George was back. George seemed to have appointed himself butler for the moment.

'Dr Stone,' he said, and with that for introduction he slipped away, leaving behind a thin, nervous looking, red-haired man.

The least he could do, Douglas felt, was to offer the newcomer a seat, so he did so. He was much less inclined to welcome the uninvited interruption to his weekend leisure. 'What brings you here?' he asked.

The abrupt enquiry seemed further to unsettle the visitor. He coloured so that the freckles which so often go with red hair faded from sight. 'I've only just heard that Stan Eastwick is dead. I had some dealings with him which are left up in the air.'

'I suppose they would be. But why come to me about it – me in particular?'

'You're the one who's at home,' Dr Stone said simply.

'That was Stan's brother George who brought you to me. I would have thought that he would have been the best person to approach.'

Dr Stone showed even more confusion. 'I – I didn't know that. He didn't let on and I asked who was the senior resident here . . .'

Although slightly flattered, Douglas was still not appeased. 'I know nothing about Stan's affairs. Two of the university staff live here, if we're talking about the same university. They may know something.'

'They would be just the people I don't *want* to know anything. Let me explain. This can be in confidence?'

'As far as I'm concerned, totally.'

'I'm senior lecturer in the Department of Botany. I've

been running a research project into the use that plants make of carbon dioxide. The carbon element is quite clear but there's a small amount of oxygen not accounted for. I've been trying to find out where it goes and how and why. But we share facilities with Zoology, and they have a bigger and better funded research project running which has a practical application. Something to do with locusts. I couldn't get any intelligent help. Stan might not be trained in scientific methods but he did know plant biology and he offered to grow and record some specimens for me. All I wanted was certain samples, with readings taken at regular intervals. I was going to pay him out of my own pocket, because to arrive at something new and to get published about it would be my next step towards promotion.'

To Douglas it seemed that an academic career was a precarious ladder to climb. 'So what's the problem?'

'The problem is that I had to lend him some expensive pieces of equipment for which I'm responsible and nobody seems to know where they've gone.'

From being an annoying intruder on a par with a buzzing bluebottle, Dr Stone suddenly became interesting. 'Would those pieces of equipment have included cylinders of carbon dioxide?'

'Yes. At least one.'

'Then,' Douglas said, 'I'm afraid you're going to have to tell the police.'

'But—'

'There are no buts. There seems to be a high probability that Stan's death may have involved what they call foul play and what you've just told me could be relevant. I am not going to be responsible for withholding evidence in a murder case. If you don't tell them I shall have to rescind my promise and tell them as much as I know. And I'm sure you can see that it will look much better coming from you. You could ask them to respect your desire for confidentiality.' And, Douglas thought to himself, a fat chance you've got.

Dr Stone must have taken Douglas's admonition to heart because DCI Laird made his appearance shortly after lunch on the day following. Douglas and Tash were doing the tedious job of transferring the files to the new system and it had seemed to be an appropriate occasion for altering the categories of the contents. It was boring work and they were glad of the excuse to stop. The three settled around the big desk.

'I gather,' said the DCI, 'that you advised Dr Stone to report to me. That was very sensible of you. But a problem follows on. There is no sign whatever of any research tools or notes around Stan Eastwick's goods and papers unless you include one medium or medical sized cylinder, which, if we go by the colour coding and a paper label, had been intended for carbon dioxide. It's in the greenhouse. What have we missed?'

Douglas said that he was sorry. 'I would love to be able to say the magic words and solve your problem, but life is rarely that easy and in this instance it's impossible. An old building like this had all kinds of holes and corners but I had most of them closed in and plastered over during the alterations. I can't believe that anybody was daft enough to plaster over a niche containing some expensive equipment, but there's nothing in the world so stupid that you can be sure that nobody's ever done it. However, Stan was a competent craftsman and George is much the same, quite capable of opening some of them up again if they knew where they were, or even of making new hidey-holes. But why should they do that, just to hide research material? He was helping out on a research project with instruments loaned by the university. If he wanted to keep them safe from a passing thief . . .'

'Yes?'

Douglas was struck by an idea calculated to keep George Eastwick busy and out of his hair for some time. 'He's on the lowest floor of the house. Some of his floor is concrete but parts of it are timber flooring on joists. He could have taken up a floorboard or two and stowed anything valuable or confidential underneath.'

'Thank you,' the DCI said. 'I knew that I could count on you.'

'Just don't let him know that I suggested it.'

SIXTEEN

Douglas lost Tash's help and company for the afternoon because her mother was busily gathering up her brood and all the necessary chattels in preparation for a visit to her sister. Then in the late afternoon the people carrier oozed quietly down the driveway and was gone. Tash and Douglas looked at each other.

'I've prepared a meal for us upstairs,' Douglas said.

Tash swallowed nervously. 'Are we doing a wise thing?' she asked.

'Whether we do it or not is up to you,' Douglas said gently. 'Either way, we have to eat. Then you can tell me what's in your mind.'

Tash nodded bravely.

The room that Douglas intended eventually to make into his dining room/kitchen was finished as far as the walls and floor were concerned, although no cooking equipment beyond a microwave oven, sufficient for the preparation of his breakfast, had so far been installed. Douglas had used the afternoon interval, during which the main kitchen was unused, to begin preparation of a simple meal, but Betty McLeish had discovered him, struggling, and had immediately divined his purpose and, approving, had taken over. Her friendship with Tash's mother did not supersede the desire in her romantic soul to aid the young lovers. There may even have been a hope on the part of one mother to score off the other. As a result a light but beautifully prepared meal was waiting upstairs, requiring only that the soup and then the main course be reheated before serving.

Champagne would have struck quite the wrong note.

Douglas had brought and chilled what he considered to be a suitable Riesling. They were sipping it while making a start on the meal when Tash said, 'I see you've put flowers on the table.'

'It seemed to be the least I could do.'

She nodded approvingly. 'I appreciate the thought. But I hope you aren't planning to produce more flowers for me, or chocolates or whatever. As I told you, this is not that sort of encounter and I don't want you to feel that I'm forcing you into a romance. We'll try me out and then think again.'

'Very sensible,' said Douglas. More and more, Tash was showing up as a sensible and self-contained young woman, wise beyond her years.

They chatted about the affairs of the day but without thinking deeply about what they were saying. When they had finished and taken coffee, Tash's manner was expectant rather than reluctant so Douglas rose and drew her to her feet, leading her in the direction of his bedroom. 'Would you rather undress privately, in the bathroom?' he asked her.

'I'm only going by what I've heard,' she said, 'but I rather thought that that was your job.'

'To undress you? Is that what you want?'

She gave a little shiver. 'Yes, I think I'd like that, to establish the mood. It would be exciting.'

In the bedroom he undressed her slowly, making a caress of each move. Her garments were clean and fresh, of good quality but not provocative. He managed to get rid of his own clothes at the same time without interrupting the process or breaking the mood. She was throwing aside her reservations. When they were both nude he took her in his arms but she crossed her own arms in front of her.

'It's not too late to change your mind,' he said.

'No, go ahead.' She seemed daunted by the size of him. She was very tense.

Douglas was not totally lacking in experience. There was sometimes a custom to write or say that a woman suffered sex in exchange for security and comfort, the assumption being that women never enjoyed the mating act. This he was sure was wrong. Each of his previous partners could surely not have been faking it, and so convincingly. If it was sometimes true, this was because the woman's partners had been selfish or unskilled. He settled down for a long period of foreplay, kissing and stroking and petting her in all the ways that a woman likes until she had relaxed and then returned his caresses. He knew that she did not want him to offer love so he whispered tributes, true as could be, to her beauty. Her eyes half-closed and her breathing quickened; her private parts softened, moistened and opened for him. He kept a generous part of his mind away from the immediate act so that he would not become too quickly and too fully engorged and therefore too large for her comfort. She returned his kisses. She no longer expected his penetration to hurt and so it did not.

He moved slowly at first until she had learned to respond. He tried to make every least motion a caress. Soon he found that he had woken a tigress. This was no passive maiden, waiting to be served. She was responding to him, move for move. She clasped him with her legs so tightly that he thought he might have to beg for mercy. In her movements against and around him he could feel her determination to give pleasure, both to him and to herself. He again used the old trick, thinking about something remote in order to postpone his own climax. Then, when he sensed that an orgasm was rushing at her, he released his own pleasure. Clasping each other tightly, they exploded in unison. She gave little squeaks of joy.

As they lay gasping in the afterglow she said, 'I had no idea.'

He said, 'Of course you hadn't. That was good. It has never been better.'

'How do you measure that?' she asked into his neck.

He said, 'We shall have to devise a formula.'

'The Young-Jamieson Formula for posterity to judge itself by?'

'Jamieson-Young. You thought of it first.'

They laughed together.

It was several minutes before he could follow Tash downstairs without betraying their secret.

SEVENTEEN

To the other residents in Underwood House there was no obvious change in their relationship. He still treated her with courtesy and disguised his instructions as requests; she continued to show him the respect due to an employer and an elder; they still laughed together at the follies of the world around them. In private, however, there were major changes. She had entered their affair in search of knowledge, determined that this would not be an affair of the heart; she had gained the knowledge but she now knew that she had been mistaken. Along with her virginity she had given him her heart and he was handling it with care. She felt that her heartbeat quickened whenever she saw him.

A question in both their minds was whether their affair had been a one-night stand or the beginning of something more lasting. Neither felt brave enough to confront the subject for fear of getting the wrong answer; but when the next day's work was done they drifted – oh so accidentally – close. Talking feverishly about something quite, quite different, they kissed and soon found themselves back on the big, soft bed. The experience was as mind-blowing as on the previous occasion. Tash never bothered to return to sleep in her own bed and she never objected to words or symbols of love.

From that moment on, there was no concealing the changed relationship. Every glance that they exchanged was so charged with emotion that even the dogs seemed to recognize it. There was a little gentle leg-pulling, but on the whole they felt that they were approved of. When Mrs Jamieson returned at the next weekend, before she had time to observe the changed sleeping arrangements, a mother's instinctive insight into her daughter's emotional development led her direct to the correct conclusion. As positively as a sheepdog, she shepherded Douglas out from among the interested observers and captured him alone in her unpretentious but comfortable sitting room.

'You and Tash have become an item, haven't you?'

Douglas had been considering how he would meet the subject. Now was the hour and he had to make a rapid choice between three possible attitudes. She did not look as stern as he had feared, nor as angry. Mrs Jamieson was proving to be a much more modern mother than he had given her credit for. Frankness was his best option.

'Yes. Not through any active manoeuvring on my part, but I'm a very willing party.'

Mrs Jamieson nodded several times. 'I won't say that I should have expected it. I knew that it was bound to come. I've been watching Tash falling for you. I would have stepped in if I hadn't been sure that you were well intentioned. You are being careful?'

'Very.'

'So far so good. Promise me, you will let her down gently?'

That came as a surprise but so also did his own reply. His thinking had not yet progressed so far. 'I have no intention of letting her down at all,' he said severely, 'and I'm surprised that you should expect it. As far as I am concerned she is now a permanency in my life. I have not yet told her so.' Even to his own ears he sounded pedantic but the occasion was one for formality.

Tash's mother sat back, her eyebrows up. 'This I did not expect,' she said. 'I trusted you to behave like a gentleman or I would never have gone away and left you together, but in this day and age one has to move with the times. I'm sorry if I'm talking in clichés but the subject is as old as life itself. I was sure that Tash would become a woman soon and I hoped that it would not be with one of these mannerless youths who seem to be taking over the world. I was relieved to see her falling for a professional, educated man. Are you thinking of marriage?'

'I'm waiting to see how Tash's mind goes. But –' Douglas's mind recoiled from a picture of Mrs Jamieson advising Tash in one direction or the other '– I am certainly not inviting you to influence her. It must be her decision. I'm twelve years older than she is. It isn't an unbridgeable gap but it's a wide one. You've brought her up incredibly well and I congratulate you. Sometimes I get the feeling that she's as mature as I am if not more so. Let's just see how things develop.'

'Yes, let's do that. But nothing is a hundred per cent safe. Suppose she were to become pregnant . . .?'

'I would offer marriage immediately.'

She smiled suddenly. 'I can begin to envisage you as a son-in-law.'

'I have been looking on you as a future mother-in-law. Happily.'

'One thing about you, Douglas, you always say the right thing. But you must be careful about the impression you give; and I depend on you to keep Tash's reputation – what shall I say? – untarnished. I'll tell you a story which you may find funny – to her dying day my mother could almost fall out of her chair laughing about it – but there's a truth buried in it.

'Between the wars, when these things were taken very seriously, my aunt was a nursing sister and it was known that she was in line for promotion to matron – senior nursing officer, they'd call it now. She was nominated to attend a nursing conference, in Paris of all places. Her colleagues thought that she had landed jammy side up, except that my sister always wore flannel pyjamas.

'Her friends insisted that she couldn't go to Paris with hairy pyjamas. What would the maid think? So they clubbed together to buy her something pink and frilly. Her train was about to leave so there was no time to do more than tuck it into her case and wave to her. She arrived safely at the conference and met some seniors over dinner, so she arranged for drinks to be put in her room and invited several quite important persons to come for a nightcap.'

As the story progressed, Mrs Jamieson's own amusement had begun to take her over and as she arrived at the climax her laughter rendered her barely coherent.

'They all went together up to her room, where the maid had unpacked her bag for her and turned down both sides of the bed, putting the frilly nightie on one side and the hairy pyjamas on the other.

'The point I want to make is that she was perfectly innocent but looked very guilty. She did not get that promotion to matron although she was later appointed SNO at a different hospital. Much of what happens to you in life may depend, not on what you are or what you do, but on what the world thinks you are and do.'

Douglas had lived through the betrothal of a brother and two cousins and as his tender secret emerged into the light of day he was expecting his life to be turned upside down with giggles and hints and controversy on such vital matters as who were going to be bridesmaids. However, that area of discussion was drowned out for the moment by a subject of more general interest. On the next Sunday morning, inconveniently early, Chief Inspector Laird arrived, insisting that all those of the household who had reached teenage years or above should hold themselves ready for a round-table discussion as soon as breakfast was past and the washing-up done.

Traces of breakfast could still be detected in the form of toast crumbs and the smell of coffee when the teenage and adult population of Underwood House assembled in the kitchen/dining room. The sky outside was black, so nobody resented the loss of their leisure time more than very slightly. Seymour McLeish had been booked to play golf despite the weather but he was glad of the excuse to remain warmly indoors and talk about murder. His wife had been hoping for a quiet day on her own but it now seemed that she must assist Hilda Jamieson in providing Sunday lunch. Professor Cullins and Hubert Campion were very smart in well-pressed slacks and shirts with cravats. George Eastwick turned up and, as usual, was making a show of bad tempter.

Tash, who knew nothing of the talk between her mother and Douglas, had seated herself firmly beside Douglas where she could feel the comforting warmth of his thigh against hers. Her mother was seated on her further side, as if to lend propriety. DCI Laird was accompanied by his sergeant and by a woman sergeant equipped with recorder and dictation book. The big room was almost crowded.

DCI Laird frowned at Tash, who had produced her own pen and shorthand book. 'Sergeant Brownie will keep the record,' he said.

Douglas smiled at him. 'We also like to keep a record,' he said.

The DCI's nostrils flared slightly as at a bad smell. 'Very well. I have asked you all to be present because we have been making little or no progress in the matter of the death of Stan Eastwick. There seems to be no doubt that he died of carbon dioxide suffocation, but beyond that we have no starting point. Usually we prefer to interview witnesses separately so that they do not influence each other's accounts, but when an enquiry refuses to get started, like this one, sometimes the only answer is to gather people together in the hope that they will refresh each other's memories.'

'And contradict each other?' Douglas suggested lightly.

'That would be a bonus,' said DCI Laird more seriously. 'Now, Mr Young, according to your own statements you and Miss Jamieson were here on the Monday and you were the only occupants to be here constantly, without a break. So you start off. Tell me all about that day.'

'A tall order,' Douglas said, 'but we'll do our best. Weatherwise I remember it as an ordinary sort of April day. Sunny with occasional clouds and a single shower around lunchtime. Tash and I were preparing a report on the Hamilton Building Society's proposal to sponsor a housing and related development on a hundred hectare site near Gorebridge. They have it under consideration now but if they consider what we wrote I doubt if they'll go ahead, so I feel free to talk about it. Our work entailed periods during which I was thinking or sketching and Tash was free to look out of the window, alternating with periods when I was dictating and we both had our heads down. Then she would be typing or doing sums on the computer while it was my turn to look out of the window. Between us I think that one or the other of us would have been looking over the back gardens for about two thirds of the time, discounting the time we spent making and eating a snack lunch.

'But what you most want to know about is the comings and goings. Of course, our office looks out to the back gardens. Anybody could have arrived at the front of the house, if they came quietly, and have walked round to the back door without being seen by either of us.

'Between eight thirty and about nine thirty, we settled down to work. During the same period most of the adult residents seemed to go off to their various businesses. Yes, Tash?'

'While I was looking out at the back, Mr George Eastwick drove off in his brother's van.'

George Eastwick gave a triumphant nod as though he had been proved right in the face of argument.

'Did you see him return?'

'No. Mr Young wanted to dictate just then.'

'Presumably,' Douglas said, 'Mrs Jamieson must have driven off in her people carrier. We wouldn't know about that – it's very quiet. She took her family with her – other than Tash, who was with me – and we knew they were back not long after lunchtime when we heard the children playing Vulcans and Borgs in and out of the trees.'

'Vulcans and Borgs?'

'From *Star Trek*,' Tash explained.

'Ah. I'm not at home often enough in the evenings to keep up with television.'

'I was shopping for clothes, mostly for the children,' said Mrs Jamieson. 'They grow at such a speed. In some ways it's been convenient, alternating boys and girls – girl, boy, girl, boy – but it does make handing down clothes difficult. And boys are so hard on clothes. Especially shoes. They'll look you straight in the eye and swear that they *never* play football on the way home from school, when one toecap is worn away and the other's hardly marked. We all had lunch in a burger bar and then we came home and we were in for the rest of the day.'

'We'll come to you in a minute, Mrs Jamieson,' said the DCI when he managed to cram a word in. (Tash's mother made a moue and mimed zipping her mouth.) 'Mr Young?'

EIGHTEEN

Douglas's brow was wrinkling of its own accord as he tried to remember details of a day that had not developed any special significance until later. 'Stan Eastwick came out,' he said at last. 'His retirement had been finalized by then and he was trying to catch up with the tidying up in the gardens, which had rather been neglected during all the kerfuffle of his retirement and people moving in. The shrub roses were overdue for pruning and he went to and fro between the roses and the greenhouse, taking cuttings I think. I lost sight of him after that except that a baker's van must have come to the front door because I heard Stan answer his door below our window and he said something about wholemeal loaves, so the man in the van must have walked round the house instead of driving round by road.'

Tasha coughed and held up her hand. 'I saw Stan again later,' she said. 'He was forking over the bed where he'd taken out the shrubs with the red berries. I think I told you about it when I made my statement.'

'You did indeed,' said the DCI. 'Did anybody answer the front door to the baker's man?'

'I did,' Betty McLeish said. 'He caught me just before I left the house to go and have lunch with my husband. There's a good little restaurant just along from the garage and if Seymour isn't lunching with anyone else we usually lunch there together. I was just getting into my little car when he arrived. It was the usual driver and our order had already been placed by phone so all I had to do was to take the money out of the box that sits on a high shelf behind the sergeant there, and pay him.'

'That's not very secure,' said the DCI. 'Anybody could walk in and help himself. Or herself,' he added fairly.

'Well, it's never happened yet. And there's never very much in it, just enough so that whoever's here can pay for any delivery that comes to the door. Nobody else came to the front door all morning except the postman and nobody need have seen him. He never rings the bell. The mail just appeared in the box at the outside front door and I suppose Tasha sorted it out and put it through the appropriate doors as usual.'

'I don't remember that particular morning but I always do that,' Tash said. Now that her relationship with Douglas was generally recognized she had begun using his first name in company. 'I'd have remembered if that day had been different. We were supposed to be going out that morning to check something but Douglas got the information he needed over the phone so we were able to stay in and get on with the report. Douglas needs to get his mail early and while I'm collecting it I may as well pop the rest of it through the letter slots. It only takes me a second or two but it can save the others a few minutes and I don't think anybody minds. I mean, nobody gets a disproportionate number of angry-looking envelopes with windows.'

'We seem to be running a public service,' Douglas said. 'But that's all right. I think that that's all I can tell you.'

'We'll see about that later,' said the DCI. 'Let's finish the morning first. Mrs McLeish, who else did you see or hear between breakfast and answering the door to the baker's van?'

'Nobody,' Betty said firmly. 'It was a very quiet morning, which was good because it let me get on with the ironing. I knew that there would only be Douglas and Tasha for lunch and they always look after themselves when they're going to be here. I just made sure that there was bread and eggs and cheese in the fridge for them.'

'Thank you. Now, Mr Eastwick. Tell me about your morning.'

George seemed to have decided that his connection, through Stan, with the university was now thoroughly broken and he was reverting to the dialect of his younger days further north. 'You a'ready heard it. Stan was pottering in the garden and greenhouse. There was naebody came 'cept Jock Swithin as works for McColm the bakers. I'd waited in for him because we was out of bread and Stan walked down to the village to gi'e his pal some seedlings. He said his pal would gi'e him dinner.'

'And what did you have for your lunch?' the DCI asked.

'I'd just had a jam sarnie when Jock rolled up, so as soon as I'd put the bread away I went out. I've been doing a wee electrical job for a wifie lives next to Seymour McLeish's garage. She told me you checked with her. I was home by around five but Stan was still no' back, least I jaloused he wasn't but I suppose he was maybe a'ready deid.' George coughed and raised a hand as though to brush away a tear. 'I made a fry-up, watched a whilie of TV and then bedded down on the Lilo on the sitting room floor.'

DCI Laird moved on. Professor Cullins and Hubert Campion had been at work in the university and several witnesses had already attested to that. They had then attended a function in the staff club – a presentation to a retiring member of the senate.

'That covers the morning – for the moment,' the DCI said. 'No doubt we shall have to return to it more than once but for the moment—'

Tash had been looking concerned. Now she looked up from her shorthand book and frowned at the DCI. 'It's not quite complete,' she said. 'You never came back to me. There's one small missing piece. I don't suppose it means anything but I'm sure you'd prefer to have the whole story.'

'No doubt about that,' Laird said. He sounded patronizing, as if to an intelligent child.

'Well, I've only just remembered something.'

'I already explained,' said DCI Laird patiently. 'That's why we're having a round-table discussion. Sometimes people refresh each others' memories.'

'Well, that's what's happened. While we've talked, the details of the whole day have been coming back to me. Mr Eastwick's van came back during the afternoon. I didn't see who was driving it, but it took the path behind the raspberry bushes as far as the greenhouse. That's a tarmac path, it's quite wide enough for the van and there's space to turn it round by the greenhouse door. It came back and drove away just a minute later. I still didn't see who was in it.'

'Well, Mr Eastwick?' said the DCI.

George Eastwick's skin had paled under its tan, ending with a grey tinge. He hesitated. 'Aye,' he said at last. 'I'd forgot, 'cause we'd done it so often afore, but the quinie reminds me. Stan asked me to fetch him a fresh gas cylinder frae the uni.'

DCI Laird exchanged a meaningful glance with his sergeant. 'Who did you meet at the university, where did you pick up the fresh cylinder and at about what time?'

George flared up – quite unnecessarily, Douglas thought.

'I'm answering nae mair dashed questions until I hae my solicitor wi' me.' He heaved himself to his feet and glared down at Douglas and Tash. 'You twa was supposed to be awa', that day.'

'I got my answer over the phone without going to look,' Douglas said.

'Ye bogger. Ye're a' fart and nae shite.' George opened his mouth and closed it again quickly. It was dawning on him belatedly that whatever he said might only be digging a deeper pit. He glared at the three officers in turn. 'You've naethin' on me,' he said. 'Naethin'. An' you'll get your heids in your hands to play wi' gin you try it on.' He turned and stumbled out of the room, slamming the door behind him.

'For the moment,' said the DCI, 'he's right. You two men go after him. Take him in. If you have to be specific, charge him with whatever comes to hand, perhaps his threatening behaviour just now. It's too early to bring up suspicion of murder. But seal up the flat downstairs and above all don't let him tamper with anything.'

The two policemen hurried out after George Eastwick. The woman officer laid down her pen for the moment and worked her right-hand fingers. The DCI watched her sympathetically. She had been doing a lot of shorthand hurriedly for quite a long time without respite. He was also taking time for thought. When she seemed more comfortable he began speaking again.

'Thank you all for being so cooperative,' he said. 'As you just heard me say, it's too early to be talking murder. Mr George Eastwick's behaviour suggests that he may be guilty of something serious but I learned years ago that if you fix too early on one suspect you may be pinning the tail on the wrong donkey. Several weeks of plodding routine may enable us to determine whether he is indeed guilty and perhaps even to prove it – if only we had the faintest idea how and why. *Why* isn't so important – the law doesn't require a motive to be proved. But *how* is crucial. Can anybody offer me the first, faint beginning of an explanation?'

There was an utter silence in the room.

'I dare say the routine processes of investigation will turn up a method. But *why*? Assuming that George Eastwick took action against his own brother, can any one of you suggest a motive?'

The silence became more total, which had seemed impossible. He sighed. 'Very well. The granny flat downstairs will be sealed and opened only for forensic examination.' He smacked his hand down on the table. 'Whatever happened

down there, traces must have been left and we . . . will . . . find
. . . them.'

It was a dramatic moment but it was followed by anti-
climax. Betty McLeish looked up at the wall clock.
'Lordy!' she said. 'Where has the morning gone? Who's
staying for lunch?'

The DCI and his sergeant agreed to accept a sandwich
apiece, which they ate at the very end of the long table.
While the residents shared a pan of curried chicken, it was
noticeable that the two officers said nothing – not, Douglas
thought, out of discretion but so as not to miss a word that
was said by the others. Douglas wished them luck. The
morning's papers had been full of a scandal involving an
MSP and an actress; the ladies of the household, with
whom Tash included herself, had no intention of discussing
anything else.

NINETEEN

For all his brave words it appeared that Detective Chief Inspector 'Sandy' Laird was still getting no further with the case. Just as a computer can arrive at answers apparently by magic, a body of people receiving information in tiny fragments and discussing those fragments can arrive at answers, some of them usually approximating closely to the truth. The word circulating among the residents of Underwood House was that George Eastwick had remained stubbornly silent. Nothing had been found pointing to method or motive and when the time allowed by the law for inquisition of suspects had run out he had been released. The phrase 'police bail' was bandied about without being properly understood. He was banned from the compact semi-basement flat, which remained sealed except when vague figures, usually in white overalls, could be seen poking around, apparently without purpose or understanding, and he was believed to be staying in Edinburgh, in lodgings approved by the police. Winnie the bulldog bitch settled down happily, sharing accommodation with Rowan.

The death of Stan Eastwick now being firmly on the back burner so far as the police were concerned, the media belatedly discovered that there was an unexplored mystery begging for attention. DCI Laird took advantage of the fresh coverage to seek the help of the public in turning up new facts, but the public on this occasion proved to be many broken reeds. The occupants of Underwood House were plagued for a while by reporters until Geraldine and Harry McLeish started feeding them with more and more far-fetched stories. After that there was peace while the media awaited developments.The small community in Underwood House could now turn its attention to the next most interesting subject, the romantic attachment of Tash and Douglas. The two persons most concerned were understood to intend marriage, although neither of them had ever quite said so, and each had a vague mental picture of slipping away to the chapel at their own places of education. Nothing so informal would be acceptable to their friends, relatives and neighbours. The bride's father, who continued to strike oil physically and metaphorically in some Arab hellhole, insisted by email that money was no object. Her mother, while uncomfortably aware of two more daughters to be provided for, refused to be the skeleton at the feast and was soon as keen as anyone to see them married in some style, in a cathedral if no palace proved to be available.

It was left to Douglas, whose profession had imbued him with a keen sense of the value of money and who was well aware of the eventual needs of two future sisters-in-law and bridesmaids elect, to put his foot down. Neither he nor Tash had any firm conviction about the existence or otherwise of a personal God so Mrs Jamieson soon found herself in tentative negotiation with a nearby very smart hotel, much patronised by local nobility, where she and Betty McLeish had been in the habit of taking coffee flavoured with a delicious sense of extravagance. Tash's residence in Douglas's flat became permanent after a single hissing argument with her mother during which Mrs Jamieson expressed anxiety about what the neighbours might think but was invited to consider just who and where were those neighbours. Like any other mother she then turned her attention to interfering in their honeymoon plans and also ensuring that Tash was provided with what she considered to be suitable underwear for such an occasion. Mrs Jamieson had been a bit of a girl in her day and if the bridegroom was already captivated there was all the more reason for keeping him so.

Meanwhile, several of Douglas's satisfied clients had been singing his praises. As a result, his practice was booming. He was driven to laying off work with a larger firm and was even negotiating with a potential future partner who conducted a similar one-man band some ten miles off. Douglas and Tash between them undertook a prodigious amount of work, somehow avoiding all the pitfalls that lie in wait for the overworked surveyor. Douglas was eagerly putting money by in order to buy for Tash an antique engagement ring with a large solitaire diamond. Tash was somewhat overawed by the prospect of carrying quite so much money on a single finger but had no intention of saying so until it was safely hers.

At such a juncture the return of DCI Laird was anticlimactic and less than welcome but they cleared an afternoon for him. The day that he first suggested had been one of Tash's days for attending college, but Tash had insisted on a change of dates. Devoted as she was to Douglas's interests she was not going to miss the next stage of a murder enquiry for anyone.

They welcomed the DCI into the palatial office with coffee and his favourite biscuits. He was accompanied only by his sergeant, explaining that he had found Tash's transcript of their previous meeting more crisp and accurate and better spelled than that of his own young lady. Would Tash again oblige? Tash realized that there was an exchange on offer. If she wished to sit in on Douglas's statement she could take the record. She sighed but opened a new shorthand book.

'I rather hope that we can keep this confidential,' Mr Laird said. 'I'm driven to come back to you because we're still in the same boat. A man died. We are fairly sure that we know what killed him. We think we know who administered it. As to how and why there are no indications at all. You know this building better than anybody. There must be something here that we have not yet found. Where,' he demanded plaintively, 'could we possibly look that we haven't yet found?'

Douglas had to struggle to keep the amusement out of his voice. 'Yes,' he said. 'I can well imagine you wanting to keep it confidential. Especially – am I right? – from Detective Superintendent Laird, your wife.'

DCI Laird flushed dully and Douglas was almost sure that he could hear the grinding of teeth. 'I would prefer that my lady wife were to know nothing of this.' Mr Laird took several deep breaths and decided to unbosom himself. 'It's a damnable position to be in. We were both up for promotion but hers came through more quickly than mine because of some little administrative hiccup over my date of birth; so now mine has to wait to be confirmed, which may not be until the next board meeting. And she's just too good about it.' DCI Laird was struggling to keep his face bland but the effort showed. 'I could understand it if she crowed, but she hasn't. A man can stand just so much saintliness. If she sees me make a mistake I can't see a smile, not even a smirk. But I know it's there just under the surface from the twinkle in her eye and the care she takes to keep the laughter out of her voice. Suppose she arrived here as my superior officer to look for whatever I've missed. Even worse, suppose she found it.'

Tash did not yet have the maturity or experience to skate lightly over the surface of such a delicate subject. 'I'm sure that if she really loves you . . .'

'Oh, she does,' said the DCI. 'That only makes it worse.' He did not explain why that made it worse, nor did either of his protagonists dare to enquire. 'I always tell my juniors to make use of any help or expertise available from the public. So for God's sake tell me what I've missed.'

There was silence for a full minute. Then Douglas said, 'I assume that you've checked the sources of supply.'

'We have indeed, without finding more than a few loose ends. He has never had an account in his own name with a gas supplier but, for instance, you knew that he's doing some work for a lady who lives close to Mr McLeish's garage and workshop. We find that he plays snooker with the workshop foreman and they go for a beer together afterwards. No law against that, of course, I wish there were, but it means that he has a ready source of refills for carbon dioxide bottles. Our forensic scientists assure me that the contents of one cylinder of carbon dioxide in that small space would be quite enough to smother somebody. Then, of course, there was the work his brother was doing for the university.'

The DCI fell silent while he considered how to go on. Douglas decided to help him out. 'So what we're all thinking is that he arrives back here in his van during the afternoon,' Douglas said. 'His information is a little out of date and he expects us to be away during working hours. He drives to the greenhouse and leaves one or more full cylinders of carbon dioxide where they'll be easily explained, removing any empty ones.

'Around sixish there's usually a sort of lull. The ladies have prepared dinner. They're taking off their pinnies and changing into something a little smarter – just in case her majesty pops round to borrow a cup of sugar – which puts an onus on us men at least to tidy ourselves up a bit but not necessarily in a more formal way, because each of us has had to remain respectable all day and I for one am becoming fed up by then of the constriction of a collar and tie or a polo-neck if it's cold weather. I usually change into fresh and well-pressed slacks and an open-necked clean shirt. The professor and Hubert do much the same.' Douglas paused. 'I hope that doesn't lead the other residents to think that I'm the same way inclined.'

Tash hid a smile. 'I think you can take it that it doesn't.'

'That's all right, then. During that lull the daylight would have been fading. Nobody would notice, except possibly

Stan himself, if George slipped out and used his van to move cylinders of gas to where he wanted them.'

'Now you're coming to the point,' said the DCI. 'Where would that be?'

'Off the top of the head, how would I know? Let's go and take a look.'

'Can I come too?' Tash asked.

'All right. But you need your coat. We'll have to go outside and there's a cold breeze.'

Tash rewarded his thoughtfulness with a glowing look.

The detective chief inspector took the hint and picked up his tweed coat. Douglas took his favourite sheepskin coat from behind the door. The trio descended the stairs – Douglas seemed to be paying particular attention to the chimney stack around which the mahogany staircase made its elegant curve.

Emerging from the front door, Douglas called a halt facing down the main drive. 'If we're on the right lines he would have gone down this drive and come back up the other one.'

'Why would he have to come to this side of the house at all?' Tash asked. 'He started and finished at the back of the house.'

There was a pause while Douglas thought back over what he had said. 'Just testing to see if you were paying attention. Anyway, we're not carrying anything heavy and I can't imagine him dropping any useful clues along the way. We'll short cut across the grass. It's quite dry.'

They rounded a corner of the house. A small group of wood pigeon, not enough to be called a flock, took off in a panic from where they had been searching for clover or for seeds blown down in the recent high winds. A walk equivalent to the breadth of a football field brought them to the screen of raspberry canes and the rhododendrons beyond which lay the tarmac path and a large greenhouse.

'A surprisingly good path for what is after all just a glorified garden shed,' said the DCI.

Douglas could not accept this slur on his ewe lamb. 'I think it's a bit more than that. The greenhouse has about the floor area of the average suburban house. It has its own boiler although that's not much used. I think Stan used to burn garden rubbish in it. The previous owners liked to have flowers in the rooms all year round. Obviously vans would need to get here occasionally with peat or dung or bags of fertiliser let alone seeds. It was a gravel path originally but I noticed that it was firm enough to be a base for tarmac so I included it when we took quotes for the driveways.'

Inside, the greenhouse contained benches supporting boxes holding everything from a fuzz of tiny seedlings to carefully separated young plants. There was a rich smell of warm compost and flowers.

'I hope you're keeping these plants watered,' said the DCI. 'They could represent a lot of money.'

'I think we've taken the right steps,' Douglas said. 'The garden centre took over the maintenance but they weren't interested in any research work and the university wasn't going to pay them. Dr Stone took away any papers and as much of the instrumentation as he could find. The flat owners get a share of the flowers in return for the garden centre selling the rest. No money changes hands.'

In a corner of the greenhouse apparently devoted to the university's work was an enclosure isolated in a polythene tent. The plants therein had obviously received little or no attention since Stan Eastwick's death. The boxes of moribund plants were enclosed in their own separate plastic tents coupled to piping that had been improvized from a garden hose. There were incomprehensible instruments for measuring concentrations of carbon dioxide. A single black cylinder lay nearby, disconnected and very lightly powdered with dust. The inspector lifted an end of it.

'Empty,' he said.

'Just as one would expect,' said Douglas. He opened the door of the small boiler and looked inside but the ashes had been cleaned out. 'We'll take a quick look at the compost heaps and then head back to the house.'

TWENTY

The DCI broke the seal and produced the key to what had been Stan Eastwick's door. The small apartment had the silence of emptiness. Douglas had expected to hear the creak of a dog leaving its basket. He found that he had to make an effort not to speak in a whisper. He led the way into the sitting room. It was very untidy, with George's airbed and nightwear lying where it had been dropped.

'Now,' Douglas said, 'we're considering the lull between work and play, the short period, around dusk at this time of year, when people are relaxing after work, perhaps having a bath or a shower, probably changing into something that will make them look and feel more leisured and ready to converse with neighbours. About this time, in fact. What would Stan and George be doing at that time? I never noticed either of them making much of an attempt at being dapper.'

'Now that you mention it . . .' Tash began. She stopped.

The two men had forgotten her presence and were looking at her in surprise. By tacit agreement they sat down in the uncomfortable garden chairs. Tash opened her dictation book on her knee.

'Go on,' said the DCI.

'I never thought about it before, but I seem to recall that George used to come back in a rush from the pub or whatever he'd been working on, just in time for a quick clean-up before eating. But the brothers didn't usually eat with the rest of us – too expensive perhaps. My mum and Mrs McLeish do most of the catering and they came to some sort of arrangement with the Eastwicks. But Stan . . .'

'Yes?' said both men.

'Let me think, now. Stan could usually be seen working around the gardens or going in the direction of the green-house until mid-afternoon. Then he'd disappear, some time between four and five. I used to assume, if I thought about it at all, that he was making a start to their evening meal. But quite often he would only be heating up a ready-made meal from the supermarket. In light evenings, he'd get back into the garden after dinner.'

'This is interesting,' said the DCI. 'You've come up against one of the walls that we've been butting our heads against. Everything points to Stan Eastwick having died during that period but we have no clue as to what he was in the habit of doing. How did you know that they took ready-made supermarket meals?'

Tash, who refused to be caught flat-footed by the question, looked at him coldly. 'I was not in the habit of dining with them, if that's what you're thinking. You can see their wheelie bin from our office windows and they are – were – often careless about putting the lid down. I noticed the cottage pie carton more than once.'

'I see. Go on.'

'That's all I had to say. Thinking back, it seemed as if Stan was always out of sight during that lull.'

'And you can't think of anything else that he might have been doing?'

Tash raised an eyebrow and wrinkled her forehead while she thought around the question. 'I can think of lots of things he might have been doing but they all seem very unlikely. At the meal, if he took it with us, or after it, he didn't seem to have smartened himself up by more than a wash and maybe changing his trousers if he'd got wet or muddy. He never shaved except first thing in the morning.'

The DCI switched his eyes to Douglas, who shook his head. 'I've no idea what he might have been doing. And we didn't move him at all when we found him,' Douglas

said. 'Did anybody comment on whether he seemed to
have been moved since he fell?'

DCI Laird frowned at the effort required in remembering.
'There were no signs reported of anybody having moved
him. The first officer to arrive was in no doubt that he was
dead and his first concern was whether he had been robbed,
so the man had the sense to look and see if he seemed to
have been searched. He didn't see any such signs and he
didn't let anyone else interfere with what was obviously
a dead body, which suggests that you found him exactly
where he collapsed.'

'Then let's go and follow in his tracks.'

They traipsed across the small entrance hall and turned
a corner. The DCI broke another seal and opened a door.
They found themselves trying to squeeze into a cramped
space which in the average house would have been expected
to fill with mops and brushes and Dysons. There was a
human outline on the floor in masking tape, becoming
rather worn. 'Did your men cart off a lot of mops and
buckets?' Douglas asked.

The DCI shook his head. 'The brothers seem to have
built another cupboard round the corner for household
tools, stealing a bit from the kitchen.'

'I wonder why.' Douglas indicated a door on his right.
'The boiler is behind there. We replaced it, of course. The
back end of this space that we're standing in was the coal
cellar but there's an oil tank now behind the hedge by the
outside door.' Douglas hummed undecidedly for a moment.
'It's very odd. Everything else in this flat is exactly as I
meant it to be, but this is somehow different.'

'Different? How?'

'Damned if I know.' Douglas opened the inner door onto
a cupboard in which a compact oil-fired boiler was
muttering. 'They're not using it as an airing cupboard either
although I suppose the new boiler's too well insulated to
be much use for that.'

'I'll have to get the forensic science laddies back to see what they can find,' said the DCI. 'Where do we go next?'

'I hope you're going to be a bit more patient with the forensic team,' Douglas said. 'If you hurry them, they'll miss what you want to know. Do you want me to tell you what to tell them to look for?'

The DCI backed out into the fresher air of the corridor, 'Am I rushing too fast? If you have something to show me, show me now.' He paused and laughed at himself. 'That sounds like a line from a song or the punch line of a rude story, I'm not sure which.'

'It could be the punch line of a very interesting story,' Douglas said. 'The old boiler was much bigger than this one. It wouldn't even have gone into this cubbyhole. For the record, the new boiler is against the bit of wall on my left. But I remember this space as going much further back so that the old boiler could connect to the chimney that runs up the middle of the staircase. This one has a balanced flue that goes out through the wall. There's a new wall across here and a new ceiling – with a plaster ventilator in it, you may care to note. I'm facing what looks like a blank wall with a digital time-clock mounted on a plywood panel but there's another time-clock half hidden behind the boiler. This space looks less than I'd envisaged it and the panel looks unnecessarily large. What's more, I haven't seen any of the digits change. I think it may . . .' There were scuffling sounds.

The DCI raised his voice. 'Just a minute,' he said. 'Don't move anything until I've had time to—'

He was too late. He was trying to squeeze past Tasha without treading on her toes or rubbing against her in too familiar a manner when Douglas backed out of the cubbyhole holding a plywood rectangle with a time-clock attached.

'Give that to me,' the DCI snapped.

'With pleasure.' Douglas handed over the plywood panel

and stepped back into the minuscule chamber. 'It hasn't been connected to anything, it was just hanging on hidden hooks. Here, I suspect, are most of the bits and pieces missing from the university.'

'Let me see—'

Douglas was enjoying himself. It is not often given to a member of the public to teach a senior police officer his job and Douglas was making the most of the chance. 'You'll see better if I turn them on.'

'Don't—'

The real back wall of the space was about a metre further back and it was shelved. On the shelves stood several CCTV monitors and Douglas had already switched one of them on. As he put his hand on a second one, the first came alive. It showed part of an empty room.

Tash had ducked under his arm. 'But that's my room. Or it was.'

The second monitor woke up. Another bedroom appeared, in full colour and sharp detail. It was a feminine room but not excessively so, papered in a modest paper of pale blue and mossy green. A lady was about to put on a cream coloured slip, preparatory to donning the dress that was laid out on the bed. Her figure looked mature but well kept and her underwear was slightly old fashioned but, though it had not been in the top bracket for extravagance, it was not unglamorous. There was machine-made lace and arti-ficial silk. Her stockings showed as little more than shadows and a faint gloss.

'Put it off,' said Tash urgently. 'Put it *off*! That's my mum.'

Douglas later told Tash, 'At least there isn't a camera in my bedroom, or if there is it's very well hidden and there's no monitor to connect to it.'

So at least their transports had not been watched by a voyeuristic gardener's brother.

TWENTY-ONE

There followed what was becoming the customary period of limbo following any major event in the Stanley Eastwick case. Unexplained, dimly seen figures carried out incomprehensible tasks. Occupants of Underwood House were rigidly excluded from the basement flat and its immediate environs, but nobody could or would stop Douglas from strolling about the house and using his eyes. He had no particular interest in criminology but he felt a responsibility for anything impinging on Underwood House and its denizens.

The DCI was no Sabbath-keeper. To him, it seemed that Sunday was a convenient day for catching people at home and without any excuses for evading him, such as the demands of their jobs. Or else he was determined to keep out of the way of his wife, who was now for the moment his superior officer. He summoned the residents to another round-table conference on another Sunday morning, but this was strictly adults only. This time he had brought his own shorthand writer. Tash's siblings had been despatched to give their grandmother the benefit of their company. The old lady, who would far rather have had her own fireside to herself for a good read of the Sunday papers, always felt obliged to make a show of being a typical granny, welcoming them with open arms, spoiling them rotten and then finding them tasks or entertainment that would keep them well out of her way for as long as was acceptable or even longer.

Douglas and Tash had made no secret of the discoveries in the basement flat, so discussion of the *cabinet de voyeur*, in tones either shocked or amused, had already been under way for several days. Discussion had been resumed but was interrupted when DCI Laird arrived and took his seat.

'I always knew that there was something sly about those brothers,' Mrs Jamieson was saying. 'If you looked at them suddenly you could catch them eyeing up a woman in a way that you mightn't like.'

'I wouldn't even like my doctor to look at me like that,' said Mrs McLeish. There came unbidden to Douglas's mind the memory of a fellow student who complained that she had been the victim of a sexual assault. Her complaints had been loud but Douglas had been sure, although he could not have pointed out a single supporting word or glance, that her description to her fellows of the event had contained the tiniest trace of a suggestion that *men, poor things, can't restrain themselves when confronted with my sexual magnetism.*

The DCI accepted a cup of coffee but without any obvious signs of gratitude. 'And you didn't think of telling me this?' he said bitterly.

Mrs McLeish put her nose up. 'I've never been one to spread malicious gossip,' she said.

'I did pass on to you what our local publican told me,' Douglas said.

The DCI opened his mouth but closed it again. After a long pause he said, 'I have just now had word that George Eastwick is on the Sex Offender Register. He was prosecuted as a peeping Tom several years ago. That pre-dated computerization and it was in a different police area, so the information only surfaced this week.'

'But,' said Tash, 'that doesn't seem like much of a motive for killing somebody, if that's what's being suggested.'

Professor Cullins remarked that many a murder had been committed over less. 'The act of voyeurism might not have furnished enough motivation in itself but it could easily have led to a quarrel that ended in homicide.' He laced his fingers together and sat back.

Douglas, once he had got past being biased by the professor's orientation, had wondered how so humdrum a man had become so senior an academic, but now he could see him in the guise of lecturer. He had authority.

'Voyeurism,' said the professor, 'is outside my field but one cannot help picking up some of the minutiae of allied subjects. Voyeurism is serious and bloody common. It usually dates from a sexual trauma while a toddler, something such as happening on a parent naked or parents having sex, and it only becomes true voyeurism when the sufferer – because he does suffer whether he knows it or not – is unable to stop but lives a life dedicated to stolen glimpses. I suppose one can understand a state of mind in which what one might call the trimmings – the courtship, the foreplay, soft lights, sweet music, words of love, exquisite liberties, stolen glimpses, lingerie, permissive touching – add up to a shining experience and the sex act itself becomes, as it is, rather ridiculous.'

Douglas struggled to keep his mouth shut. The idea of being instructed about sex by a known homosexual was mad and yet his words were making sense.

The professor continued. 'Now, imagine two brothers, brought up strictly, the elder bloody desperate with desire but frustrated by the inhibitions of the era. Then perhaps the elder commits a sex act on the younger. This is only hypothesis but it seems highly probable. What could be more likely than that the brothers should share, perhaps even infect each other with the alternative pleasure of the voyeur? They grow up sharing that substitute for real sex. To add to all the other tensions between them, the younger may be holding the threat of complaining to the police over his elder. Some recent German research suggests that jealousy over the target of rival peeping bloody Toms can become just as bitter as jealousy between physical lovers.'

Betty McLeish and Tash's mother, the two most likely

targets of the voyeurism, were looking mortified. Douglas decided that it was high time that the discussion was given a new twist. 'And, of course,' he said, 'during the later stages of the work on this house, Stan Eastwick was here, there and everywhere, lending a skilled hand with those small jobs that fell outside the building contract. His brother was only helping him out from time to time.'

Hubert Campion was never an outspoken person, preferring to listen and nod and smile, but he found his voice. 'Stan was the one who always seemed to be about the university buildings. He must have been responsible for the thefts, so at least he knew about them.'

'But I still don't understand,' Tash said. 'They can't have been putting cameras all round the place. Unless they were hidden in things, James Bond style.'

The professor smiled at her innocence. 'My dear, you may have been watching too many old films. The modern digital video camera can be amazingly small. If you're not too fussy about fine detail there are the Skype webcams that they sell in supermarkets for around a fiver for the set. The lens part of one of those is about the size of the top of a pencil. You could hide it in a keyhole. In reality shows they hide them in buttons and billiard pockets and the fittings of handbags and briefcases and they produce remarkably sharp images. But in point of fact my lady colleagues in zoology, who you might expect to welcome such toys for the intimate study of insects and small animals, aren't too enamoured of them. One lady admitted to me that she liked to use one to tidy her back hair and that was all.'

Douglas had brought a set of the architect, Harris Benton's drawings with him. 'The wiring could go down the former flue which is now disused.'

The DCI was uneasy at discussing the technicalities of murder with the witnesses but he was not going to cut off the flow of useful information. His eyes were always on whoever was speaking. 'How would the carbon dioxide have been introduced?' he asked.

Douglas found the answer ready for his tongue. 'I noticed a small patch of cement beside the outside door of the flat. It's coloured to blend in with the stone so you have to look at the textures to find it. I think you'll discover that a hole was drilled through the stone and a pipe – flexible plastic ventilation pipe or plain garden hose – led to the ventilator beside the . . . what shall we call it? The voyeur's cabinet. Somebody could have backed his van up to the door and led a piece of pipe direct to the hole where the patch is now. It wouldn't matter if Stan heard the gas hissing in. The door to the voyeur's cabinet could have been locked from outside, sealing him in.' Douglas, infected by the professor, was aware that the scansion of that last sentence was awry and nearly inserted an imprecation to rectify it. 'He wouldn't have had time to write a note, there's no keyboard and anyway George had most of two whole days to tidy away anything like that.'

'Now I can tell our SOCOs what to look for,' the DCI said with satisfaction.

This feast of reason was interrupted by the sound of a vehicle and a very smart Range Rover passed into and out of view on its way to the door. Tash went out, returning with a smart and attractive lady in expensive tweed. Tash had a noticeable twinkle in her eye. 'Detective Superintendent Laird,' she announced.

The men all rose. They might not have done so for any other female police officer, on the assumption that any woman enrolling as an officer had sacrificed any desire to be regarded as a weak and dependent citizen, but Superintendent Laird was different. She had been a lovely girl and remained an exceptionally beautiful woman. Her attraction was accentuated by the fact that she seemed quite unaware of it. She had the unconscious authority that goes with breeding, education and money all combined. The

DCI was first up on his feet.

Douglas felt the imp of mischief waking. 'Honeypot, I presume,' he said, offering his hand.

She looked at him coldly but shook it at arm's length and then accepted the proffered chair. They all sat. Only by a twitch of one eyebrow did she admit to being sensitive about a nickname that had been an obvious pun on her maiden names but would by now have been left far behind had it not been so appropriate.

She addressed her husband. 'I came to join you,' she said, 'not because you need supervision but because I have some fragments of news that I'll drop in at the appropriate moment. I've read the reports on this case up to today, so if you give me a quick resume of what has been said this morning I'll be up with you.'

Her husband obliged with a succinct and precise summary of the morning's disclosures. Douglas noticed that he gave full credit for any useful observation or reasoning, which in his experience showed unusual generosity.

She listened intently. 'Yes,' she said, 'I can see why you consider George Eastwick the prime – indeed probably the only – suspect. And here comes the first titbit of fresh information. You left orders that he was to be picked up and brought in. But it seems that the woodentops – I really must stop calling them that, they resent it – haven't been able to find him. He has not been at his approved lodgings since yesterday evening. He may walk in with an innocent explanation for his absence but that seems unlikely. If he has fled, that itself is evidence of guilt. And that raises two subsequent questions. One, where has he gone? And, two, how did he know at this precise moment that his guilt was about to be revealed?'

The silence was only broken by a sharp intake of breath. Douglas felt compelled to give the residents a lead. 'Does any one of us have any ideas on question two? How did George come to know that the wrath of God was about to fall on him? Has anybody had contact with him?'

His question was answered by a chorus of headshakes and negatives. The DCI's shorthand writer, however, was becoming very red in the face. She was young, quite pretty if buck teeth were ignored and she had been a silent listener. When she spoke she revealed a strong accent that could only have come from within twenty miles of Sauchiehall Street. 'That could be my fault, ma'am,' she said. 'I hope it's not but it could. George Eastwick phoned for Mr Laird yesterday, wanting a word with him. He wanted to know when he'd get back into his home. I said that Mr Laird was having a special meeting today and I was sure that Mr Eastwick would be hearing something by tonight.'

DCI Laird said, 'Come and see me tomorrow morning,' and his voice was cold.

'That gives us a very likely answer to question two,' said Honeypot. 'With possible relevance to question one, I'll give you another piece of good news. An email was waiting this morning but you were in too much of a hurry to open it. Your promotion is through at last. They don't want us falling over each other so, although we're to be flexible about this, I'm to stay with Edinburgh and the Lothians and you are to look to the Borders. Congratulations. And we are to be ready to face the media together tomorrow morning, ten a.m.'

A congratulatory grunt went round the table.

'Thank you,' said Mr Laird. By the slope of his shoulders and the stillness of his hands Douglas knew that he was beginning to relax. 'I'm happy to know it. But why did you choose this rather strange moment to reveal all.'

Honeypot smiled. 'Because that makes this my case. There is to be a gradual transfer of responsibilities. I remain in Edinburgh and the Lothians – mostly, I think, so that I can retain control of the dog unit – and you remain based in Edinburgh but with special responsibility for the Borders.'

'I wish you more luck with this case than I've had,' said her husband. 'Is that all?'

'Almost.' She glanced round the interested faces. 'It will come out at the press conference so there's no point being coy about it just now. The powers felt that two Superintendent Lairds would be one too many and could cause confusion. It is strongly suggested that I revert to using my maiden name. So I am Superintendent Honoria Potterton-Phipps. But I really think that we could drop the Phipps professionally. How does that grab you?'

'Not uncomfortably,' said her husband. 'When we first met, you were Detective Sergeant Potterton-Phipps, aka Honeypot. Now that you're no longer my superior officer I can start calling you Honeypot again.'

'Not that you ever stopped.'

'I suppose,' Douglas said, 'that a congratulatory drink would be out of order?'

Both the senior officers smiled. 'I'm afraid so,' said Honeypot. 'Ask us again when you're no longer witnesses in an active case.'

When Superintendent Potterton had been shown the secret voyeur's cabinet and the officers had departed, Tash and Douglas had a moment of privacy.

She said, 'Never mind. They can come and dance at our wedding.'

'You've changed your mind about getting married?' Douglas said. 'Or is this your oblique way of telling me something?'

'It's my oblique way of telling you that we have a young Young on the way. Don't squeeze me quite so hard or you'll damage Douglas Junior. That's better.' She produced a joyous grin. 'Everybody told me that nothing is a hundred per cent safe. I believed them but thought that I was probably the stork-proof exception. The surgery phoned me my test results yesterday. We must have rung the bell on the very first shot. Now, come and help me search the bedroom again. I want to be quite sure that we're not going to figure on somebody's candid camera.'

'I have already done that,' Douglas said. 'Twice.'

TWENTY-TWO

The disappearance of George Eastwick following the unexplained death of his brother caused a minor and short-lived stir in the media. The flatholders in Underwood House were troubled for a while by the intrusion of reporters but all mention of voyeurism, which would have been meat and drink to the tabloids, had been carefully expurgated so that a brief resurgence of interest, which had been roused when *Crimewatch* had made mention of the desire of the police to discuss with George the death of his brother, began to die again. No very good photograph of him had been produced and, although at first glance the feeling had been that he would soon be found, it was realized that a short haircut, the removal of some facial hair and adoption of a determined smile would allow him to mingle unnoticed with the men in almost any Scottish street.

Absorbing though the vanishing of George Eastwick may have been to those in Underwood House, the approaching nuptials of Tash and Douglas soon took first place. A comedy had been shown on TV that finished with the presumably happy couple, their parents and the priest, standing unaccompanied in the middle of a field. Substitute a registrar for the priest and Douglas felt that the scenario had much to commend it. Their friends and family, however, threw up their hands in horror at the prospect of being deprived of the excuse for a good party at the expense of a man who was doing very nicely out of Arab oil; and Tash was easily persuaded to their viewpoint. Summer had almost trickled away during the many stops and starts of the Eastwick case. Some of Tash's relatives were understood to be straight-laced and it seemed possible that Tash might be embarrassed by an early appearance of bumps and kicks, so a date in September was chosen and arrangements were agreed with the hotel and the registrar.

A wedding, it seemed, was simplified little if at all by the transfer from church to hotel. One journey by bridal car was obviated but routines that were everyday to a church ceremony had to be considered afresh. Any attempt to involve Douglas in all the work was countered by his pointing out how busy he was in his professional life. This was valid, but was accompanied by the snag that poor Tash was just as heavily engaged on Douglas's business in addition to being the obvious person both to make decisions and to implement them, all this while carrying her extra burden. All the three loads upon her small person, however, were gladly taken up. Everything that she wanted out of life was being gifted to her. Douglas found her typing left-handed a list of those who simply had to be invited while in the other hand she held the telephone over which she was ordering flowers.

The small team of police had gradually been whittled away as lead after lead had been found to go nowhere. A mere detective inspector had been bossing around the few remaining officers until eventually it appeared that the Eastwick case had been solved and that the only missing element was the proof that might eventually be found along with the guilty man. The case was consigned to a high shelf, to await that or any other new break.

It came as a surprise, therefore, when Honeypot herself arrived unaccompanied in an even newer Range Rover and asked for a word with Tash. Douglas joined them at Tash's request. They settled in Douglas's small sitting room with coffee on the low table.

'I had the feeling,' Honeypot said, 'that if I sent a more junior officer to discuss this matter you might feel that we were not taking it seriously, but I can assure you that we are taking it very seriously indeed.

'Enquiries into George Eastwick have been continuing but the information has been reaching us in drips and drabs. However, it does reach us in the end and we don't like the way it adds up. Before Mr Eastwick vanished he was in approved lodgings and he was inclined to take a drink. In his cups, he let a few things slip that his fellow lodgers have quoted to us.

'We already knew that he is not short of money. He had owned his flat in Falkirk outright – he sold it without difficulty for a very good price and that money disappeared along with him.

'He also has a source of information. I thought that we had closed off one leak coming out of the police, but apparently not completely. If you have money, you can buy information. He satisfied himself that you two, and particularly you, Miss Jamieson, were responsible for high-lighting the facts that have brought him into so much trouble. Why he singled out you in particular remains a mystery. He is a man filled with hatred and just now that hatred seems to be focussed on you.'

'It . . . it beats me,' Tash said. She seemed undecided whether to give Douglas the credit or to accept the threat to herself.

Douglas felt his mouth go dry. 'You would have got there eventually without any help from us,' he said.

'Possibly, although it was your familiarity with the building that led you to it. Anyway, you should put that argument to him rather than to me.'

Douglas and Tash exchanged a look. Hers was fright-ened, his was more surprised. 'But what can he do?' Tash asked. 'Would he dare to show his face around here again?'

'Not if he has any common sense,' said Douglas.

'The question,' said Honeypot, 'is whether he does have any sense, common or otherwise. It may well be argued that to be filled up with hatred leaves no room for sense. From reports, the man was barely rational even earlier. To kill his own brother in order to gain possession of the *cabinet de voyeur* or out of a quarrel arising from the same cause, seems hardly rational. And then to see his capital melting away while struggling to stay one jump ahead of the police could easily push him over the brink. But, as I'm sure you know, an irrational person can show great cunning on subjects outside their immediate obsession.

'To attempt an answer to your questions, Miss Jamieson, if he has changed his appearance, yes, he might well dare to show his face around here. And something else very serious has come belatedly to my attention. There has been much talk lately about uniting all the Scottish forces into one police force. I can see the difficulties but they should be faced, or else a much more efficient means of sharing information should be devised.'

'When you become chief constable,' said Douglas, 'you can make that proposal, but that would undoubtedly land you with the job of devising and introducing it.'

Honeypot looked at him suspiciously for a moment, wondering whether the suggestion had contained an element of sarcasm, but apparently she was satisfied. 'Well, thank you. It has taken all this time for the information to reach me that Mr Eastwick has a firearms certificate, issued by a different police force, on which he holds a point two two three rifle for the control of roe deer. He had left it in the care of an Edinburgh gunsmith who knew nothing of his troubles. I don't know if Mr Young knows anything about rifles—'

Douglas had belonged to a stalking family. 'Point two two three? Very high velocity,' he said. 'Flat trajectory. Pinpoint accuracy.'

'You do, then. That rifle was collected. Mr Eastwick's van was found in the car park at Perth railway station. He could be anywhere by now. If he has stolen a replacement

vehicle we may find him through that; if he has purchased
one it may be much more difficult and, if he's using public
transport, even if there weren't enough men carrying
bagged rifles for the stalking he would only need a large
golf bag. Any man carrying a gun case or a golf bag is
being stopped, but so far without result.'

Douglas gripped Tash's hand more tightly. He could feel
her trembling. 'So where do we go from here?' he asked.

'That,' said Honeypot, 'is exactly what I was going to
ask you. You get married in about ten days, I believe?'

'True,' said Douglas. Tash just smiled.

'I suppose it's too much to hope that you're going for
a long honeymoon somewhere a long way away?'

'We intend to visit my mother,' Douglas said. 'That
seems to be inescapable. She's in sheltered housing near
Aberdeen. She has the early stages of Alzheimer's.
We've considered bringing her down here but she won't
move. That's quite understandable. All her friends are
up there. After that, we plan to tour – in Britain, if the
fine weather lasts. Tash feels that she's never seen much
of her own country.'

'I couldn't persuade you to defer the visit to your mother,
could I?'

'I'm afraid not.'

'I've never met Douglas's mother,' Tash explained. 'She
doesn't travel but she's always wanted to see Douglas
married. All our other friends and relations are around
here. The best compromise seemed to be to make an immediate visit, tell her all about it and give her a copy of the
video.'

'I can see where this is leading,' said Douglas. 'I was
sure that George came from up that way. My father's last
posting was in Aberdeen so I spent some years there and
I was certain that I recognized the accent.' He was tempted
to give a little lecture on the origins of the Doric language.
Tash was always avid for fresh knowledge. But this was

not the time. 'He would find it easiest to melt into the background where his accent was the norm.'

Honeypot was leaning back in her chair. She was obviously deep in thought although her smooth brow remained unfurrowed. 'There have been sightings of him reported from Aberdeenshire, but no more than for anywhere else. That's what you always get with such an uncertain description and a rotten photograph. I hope that we've stopped any more leakage of information but I can't be sure – we have less control over civilian employees in headquarters than over serving officers. On such vague grounds I'd hardly feel justified in asking you to change the date of your wedding or your planned visit to your mother. And I'm sure you'll appreciate that we do not have the resources to provide you with a bodyguard; and if you could afford three people full time – because that's what it takes – you wouldn't be working so hard in a small way of business. But there is the possibility that he might become aware of your presence in Aberdeenshire and follow you up. Could I suggest that you make your visit a quick one and then hop on a cruise ship for the rest of your honeymoon?'

Tash and Douglas conferred by a quick glance. 'If we could get a late booking, without having to take a whole suite on a Cunarder, we could go along with that,' Douglas said.

'I'll find out about bookings and get back to you. Meanwhile, stay away from lit windows, keep your car closer to the front door and if somebody produces police identification and says to come quickly, don't argue about it, just come. Have a good look first at the identification and don't hesitate to phone me if you have any doubts.'

Honeypot got up and smoothed her skirt over her perfect hips. 'One more thing. You have a certificate with two shotguns on it. You are legally entitled to hold those guns. You may legally carry them, within certain restrictions that I'm sure you know about. If you point them at anybody you will be taking a serious risk of being in the wrong or, indeed, of giving him a legal right to shoot you. Think about that. If you shoot somebody in self-defence you will initially be in the wrong, the burden of proof will be on you and it will be my regrettable duty to arrest you. You may or may not be acquitted. The law may say that you should have waited for a properly authorized officer to rescue you. And the law is the law, whether I agree with it or not.'

When the Range Rover had pulled away with a deceptive smoothness that spoke of a considerable expenditure above the usual purchase price, Douglas led Tash back to his sitting room. Without releasing her fingers he sank into one of the deep chairs and pulled her down onto his knee.

'This calls for a little discussion,' he said.

Tash wriggled into a more comfortable and affectionate position. 'No, it doesn't.'

'Tash, sweetheart, I can't bear to put you in any danger. We could postpone our wedding until they've caught him.'

'No,' said Tash. 'No. I don't want that.'

It cut Douglas to the heart to see her distress but he continued, 'Tash, I can't take chances with our happiness. I think we're both happier now than we've ever been.'

She struggled up to her feet. 'I was. But now I think you're afraid of committing yourself. Is that it? Have you got cold feet?' She fought to speak calmly but there was a sob in her voice. 'Or have you gone off me already? Is the honeymoon over before it's even started?'

She had the look of a troubled child and he was reminded how young she was. He knew that this could be serious and yet he wanted to laugh.

He jumped up, grabbed her by the elbows, dragged her into his arms and spoke urgently. 'Silly sausage! There's nothing in the world that I want more than to be married to you. But that bad bastard is threatening you. I shan't sleep easily while he's on the prowl. I think we're safe here if we take a little care, but as soon as we start travelling around we could be easy meat. My mother's in the phone book, for God's sake! Did you arrange for the wedding to be videoed?'

She nodded. 'But it's a very short ceremony.'

'That doesn't matter. Perhaps we could get away for the moment with putting a greeting message from each of us onto the same DVD and sending it to her with a promise to visit later.' There were tears on her cheeks and, well aware that he was living a cliché, he began kissing them away.

She seemed comforted but still adamant. 'No,' she said. 'That wouldn't do. You'd have to give her a jolly good excuse and I can't think of a better one than the truth; but she'd be worried sick if you told her that there was somebody after us with a rifle. I'm just trying to imagine myself as an old woman with Alzheimer's disease, not understanding why my son won't bring his bride for me to meet.'

Douglas was about to suggest that they could plead some non-life-threatening illness for one of them when the buzzer of the entryphone sounded. Still wound together they walked to answer it.

A voice said, 'Mr Young? I'm from Lothian and Borders Police, Technical Division. Superintendent Laird instructed that I sweep your flat for bugs.'

Douglas said, 'Bring your identification up with you,' as Tash pressed the button.

'There you are,' Tash said. 'Honeypot doesn't mean to let anything happen to us.'

The man, when he had brought his boxes of tricks upstairs, was small and pop-eyed. He found nothing but he said, 'I'll be back. I don't necessarily find them if they're not switched on at the time, and there can be new ones put in later. But you're clean for now.'

His identification was indisputable. Earlier, it had been

his job to report on the video set-up between the bedrooms and the basement flat which, he said, had been ingenious and almost up to professional standard. Tash and Douglas felt that his admiration was misplaced.

TWENTY-THREE

During the run-up to the wedding, Douglas refused to be seen taking more than the most obvious and basic precautions against making life easy for a sniper. He knew that Honeypot was taking what precautions limited manpower would allow but he preferred not to remind Tash of the threats. Unknown to her he was slipping out of the house around dawn and dusk, carrying one of his shotguns loaded with heavy shot, to slip quietly through the woodland strips surrounding the house and gardens. Several times from the cover of a favourite clump of rhododendrons he saw an unmarked police car cruise slowly past and twice an officer got out and circled the house. Such visits might not prove very efficacious but they might well add up to a deterrent.

When Tash remarked that he did not seem to be taking the threat too seriously he retorted that she never stood still for long enough to give a sniper a chance. There was some truth in this. She was labouring to ensure that Douglas's paperwork for his clients would be wholly up to date. At the same time, while Tash's mother was satisfied that she herself was performing all the duties proper to the mother of the bride, every decision and the resulting action was referred to Tash.

The father of the bride had returned from the Middle East but was little help. His contribution seemed mainly to consist of remembering ever remoter relatives who simply had to be invited. A high proportion of these accepted and when the hotel's bedrooms were fully booked it was left to Tash to find accommodation for them elsewhere. A halt was called only when it was clear that the hotel's dining room could not possibly accept even one more diner.

All in all, it was a relief when the great day dawned. Autumn in Scotland can be fine, warm and colourful, and this was just so. Rowan was bestowed in kennels but was not more than mildly disappointed, having been there before. Winnie, Stan Eastwick's bulldog, had been left behind when George made his getaway and was handed over to Douglas, who had become mildly fond of the bitch, for safe-keeping. She also went into the kennels but seemed comforted by Rowan's company. Douglas's BMW, with empty suitcases on display, stood outside the hotel, ready to be decorated by his friends. Behind the hotel and screened by wheelie bins was a fast but inconspicuous grey Ford hired in strict confidence from Seymour McLeish, who had the keys and would take the BMW into his care as soon as the couple had made their escape. Unfortunately, in his haste, Douglas had chosen a car unseen from the list of vehicles traded in and now available for sale, only satisfying himself that the car had a valid current MOT certificate. Nobody mentioned that it had little chance of getting another one.

A civil ceremony can be very short. There was only the briefest music to accompany the bride's entrance to the ballroom and the couple's exit. There was much kissing and handshaking. The dining room was lavishly decorated with tasteful floral arrangements. It was filled with guests. The meal was excellent although the soup could perhaps have done with a touch more paprika. The speeches went well in an atmosphere of great jollity but were interrupted when the younger bridesmaid was smacked for flicking pats of butter across the room. The bride's father told a story about a couple on the verge of their golden wedding who announced that they were to be divorced. There was horror in the family and an outburst of phone-calls. 'Well, it worked,' said the husband. 'They're all coming to

persuade us to stay together, for the sake of the grandchil-
dren. *And this time they're paying their own fares!*'

When it was understood that the couple were about to
leave the company assembled on the tarmac around
the much decorated BMW, nobody paid any attention
to the grey Ford that skirted the side of the hotel
and took to the back drive.

They had left in good time, but Douglas had not been able
to avoid a few drinks and so Tash, who had only recently
passed her test, was driving. In an unfamiliar and more
powerful car she was not the most confident of drivers and
she did not have the experience to explain that the car
handled very badly. They were in no great hurry; nor were
they hungry.

'Is it just my inexperience talking or is this a damned
awful car?' Tash asked.

'It is damned awful, as you say. Seymour was busy so
he just handed me a list and said, "Tell Charlie which one
you want." I don't think Charlie realized at the time that
anybody was proposing to drive the thing and I just checked
that it had an MOT certificate and was taxed and insured.'

'Well, Charlie should be ashamed of himself.' Tash was
silent while she slowed to let a tanker overtake. Then she
said, 'Isn't Charlie the one that George Eastwick was
buddies with?'

'I think you're right.'

'Well, that's just dandy. So George probably knows
exactly what car we're in as well as where we're going.'

They came off the motorway and stopped for a snack
at Kinross. They spent the night in Perth and then took
what had once been the main road, slightly encumbered
by small towns and restricted to sixty miles per hour, but
shorter and safer than the notorious dual carriageway to
Aberdeen which they rejoined for a few miles before cutting
off in order to climb over the Cairn o' Mount. Before that

climb, however, Tash noticed one of the yellow, short-term signposts that are used for passing events such as game fairs and pop concerts.

'What's happening at Straloch Moor?' she asked.

Douglas had been preoccupied after observing a brown van that had been two, three or four vehicles behind them for some miles, visible in the door mirror on his side of the car, but he realized suddenly that he was being offered an opportunity. 'Turn off. We can go that way. There was something about it in the paper,' he said. 'There was a very rare blue grouse seen there. That's an American bird. It's not known for its long distance capability so they think it must be a fugitive from a private collection. The twitchers are getting excited about it.'

Tash slowed, signalled and made the turn. 'Those are the people who tick off the birds they've seen in notebooks, aren't they? Do people still do that?'

'It's harmless and healthy and it keeps them off the streets. It may have been coincidence, but I think we're being followed.'

'The brown van?'

'Yes.'

'I wondered about it. Do you want to drive?' Her voice shook slightly but he was delighted by her cool resolve.

'Not yet.'

Suspicion was becoming a habit with Douglas. In the let-down after all the fuss and flapdoodle, Tash was basking in the happiness of having achieved her one desire – marriage to Douglas. He, on the other hand, now that he was out from under what he believed to be Honeypot's protective shelter, could not keep his ever active mind from turning over and over the permutations of what the next day or hour or minute might bring. Half expecting an ambush, he had laid his two shotguns, in their bags, on the back seat and he had a handful of cartridges in his jacket pocket. He thought about using his penknife to make a ring of cuts around a cartridge between the propellant and the shot, transforming it into a formidable and longer-range weapon where the shot-filled end separated off and flew as a solid missile. But if he attempted such surgery in the car, which was bouncing over what was degenerating into a farm track, he would probably cut his wrist, severing his hand.

Douglas had one big advantage. While he was a student, a small legacy had enabled the purchase of his first motor-cycle, and in the thrill of novelty he had explored every little-known road or track that he could find within a day's run of Aberdeen. If only he had a photographic memory and total recall of that track instead of a vague recollection. It had been passable for a motorbike and might accept a car, but he doubted very much if the van could pass that way. Or was he being paranoid? Was the presence of the van a mere coincidence?

Sheep hurried out of their path. He was reminded that somewhere along here there was an isolated farm where a farmer scraped a living by running sheep in the grass and heather. A drastic plan crept into his mind. If indeed the presence of the van were coincidence, not very much harm might be done. If not . . . they would see what they would see.

Before he had time to think it out they came over a crest and the farmhouse stood up beside the road, stark and unyielding. It looked as though it had been abandoned leaving the remaining sheep to manage and breed if they could. 'Turn round past the house,' he snapped. 'Stop dead. And then move over. I'll drive.'

Obediently – and Douglas sent a prayer of thanks To Whom It May Concern, that he had been granted a wife who could do the right thing immediately and argue after-wards if at all – Tash swung round the gable of the farm-house and skidded to a halt. Douglas was already out and running.

The driver of the brown van came over the crest to find
a figure in his path with a gun to its shoulder, aimed at
his head. There was a bang and his windscreen became a
myriad splinters of glass but it stayed in place. Douglas
was ready to dive over the low, dry stone wall if necessary,
but the van swerved onto the humped and overgrown
heather. On the downhill slope with the heather rolling
under his tyres, it took him ten seconds to pull up.

Douglas piled into the car and drove back over the crest.
Tash was right, the car did handle badly. It put him in
mind of steering a wild elephant backwards by its trunk,
not that he had ever attempted that feat. His limbs were
shaking and his mouth was very dry.

They hit the major road not far south of their intended
turn-off. Douglas drove with one eye on his mirrors until
he had made the turn. Tash must have reacted similarly
because it was just as his breathing returned to normal that
she said, 'Was it George?'

'I thought so, that's why I fired. I still think so, for all
the glimpse I got of him. I bloody well hope so, anyway.
And it wasn't a plain van. It was a camper though with
that dark colour and darkened windows you could hardly
tell. By the time he gets it back on the road he won't know
which way we went. Get my mobile phone out of my
pocket and phone Honeypot. Tell her what happened.'

He listened with half an ear while Tash gave a remarkably accurate and unemotional account of what had
occurred. Concluding the call, Tash said, 'She wants us to
carry on as planned but to keep her posted.'

From a call phone in their home village, Douglas had
booked a room in a fishing hotel overlooking one of the
best stretches of the Aberdeenshire Dee but so secluded
by woods that few people other than addicted salmon
anglers knew that it was there. Honeypot had recommended
it. The salmon would not be running for some weeks yet
so that the rates were not at their vertiginous highest.

They were expected. Their room was all that it should
be. Tash was her usual loving self. She put Douglas's
lacklustre love-making down to tiredness. It had been a
long day.

Breakfast next morning was designed to give stamina to
a man who was going to spend the day standing in the
river with ice floes nudging his bottom. Douglas was unsure
what the day would bring so he stoked up with bacon,
eggs, mushroom and black pudding and encouraged Tash
to do the same.

There had been no signs of a hostile presence but Douglas
was anxious to escape from where his movements might be
predictable. He settled their bill and stowed the car with both
of his shotguns (already loaded, contrary to all good safety
practice) in the back of the car, where they were hidden behind
two suitcases but quickly accessible from under a rug.

He was slightly ahead of his time. As instructed, he had
phoned Honeypot to report their safe arrival and had been
told that an officer from the Grampian force would join
them at ten sharp. They waited for a few minutes on a
settle facing a log fire in the hall.

'What will your mother think of me?' Tash whispered.
'Will she think me not good enough for you?'

'I'm not sure that she'd consider Her Gracious Majesty
good enough for her baby boy. She would probably
accept the Archangel Gabriel as a reasonable second
best.'

'Really?'

'No. Not really. I think she's been worried in case I'm
of the professor's persuasion. She's been so keen to see
me married that she would welcome Lucretia Borgia into
the family.'

'Who?'

'Never mind.'

A single, tough-looking plain clothes officer arrived
within a few seconds of the planned time. He introduced

himself and showed his identification, confirming that he was Charles Ziegler, a member of the Armed Response Unit. He looked enormous, but that, Douglas soon decided, was due to a loose suit of heavy tweed under which all sorts of weaponry could have been concealed. Douglas suspected that he was also wearing light body armour but that he might have been bulletproof without it. His partner, he said, was off sick.

'I've to meet a trade delegate at Dyce Airport at the back of four,' he said. His tone made it quite clear that compared to Douglas and Tash a trade delegate was important. 'You pay your visit. I'll make sure that the outside's clear. Tell me now what time you're going to leave and I'll see you on your way for as long as I can.'

'I was planning to get away at about twelve thirty,' Douglas said.

Ziegler nodded. That time was now set in concrete. 'Away you go,' he said. 'I'll follow you.'

Mrs Young had her own bungalow in an attractive sheltered housing complex on the other side of the river and about five miles nearer to Aberdeen. The different units were clearly signposted. For the first time since leaving their wedding hotel they were where they might have been expected and Douglas felt exposed. He could see that Tash had been suddenly reminded of George Eastwick and his threats but she bore herself bravely. As he pulled up at the door he saw Ziegler park a heavy looking Mercedes where he had both the car and the door in view.

Mrs Young came to the door. It took her several seconds to identify Douglas. The family had been warned that although her dementia was at an early stage her short term memory was already affected; but she looked hale, her colour was good and for the moment only a tremor in her hands betrayed her failing health. She was shorter than Douglas but she tried her best to envelop him in a big hug.

She managed better with Tash, who was of much the same height as herself. 'So you're Natasha,' she said. 'My new daughter. Come away in.'

She brought them into a small, cosy sitting room with a pleasant outlook towards the river. Coffee things were already on the low table with a percolator bubbling quietly on the floor and out of harm's way. She had a struggle to lift the percolator, which had evidently been filled to more than its usual capacity in honour of the visitors.

When all three were sipping at a coffee which, considering the rituals that had gone into its preparation was surprisingly awful, she had to be regaled with details of the wedding, who had been there and what the ladies had worn. Douglas promised more than once that she would be sent a DVD of the whole wedding, including speeches. Her small TV had no viewing facility but there was a DVD player, she said, in the common room and all the other ladies loved a wedding. She was quite happy in her sheltered home, she said, and she had both friends in the home and visitors who still remembered her and Douglas's father. But she was not allowed to cook for herself apart from making hot drinks, because of the shakiness of her hands, which made it impossible to give them lunch. If she had had more warning . . .

Douglas avoided mentioning that she had had several weeks of warning. They had to leave soon, he said, to catch a plane from Dyce. Friends were expecting them.

'But you will bring . . .' She stopped, searching for Tash's name.

'Tash.'

'No . . .'

'Natasha.'

She lit up. 'That's it! Natasha! We haven't had time for a proper chat. You will bring her back again?'

'Yes, of course I will, Mother. We'll make a much longer visit next time, picking the weather. If business goes well

I might even come for a week's fishing on the Dee and you can have her with you all day.'

His mother smiled sweetly. 'I'm sure I'll like that, dear. I always wanted a daughter to talk girl things with. Make it soon. Goodbye – er . . .' She had forgotten Tash's name again.

Douglas got back on the North Deeside Road. There was some other traffic but nothing that he considered significant. Ziegler was following but staying well back.

It would soon be clear to any follower that, instead of going back by the road on which they had arrived, he was heading for the road by Braemar and over Glen Shee. It was a long road and as soon as they had crossed the old boundary into Tayside what had been a straightened road suddenly reverted to a twisting switchback through wild looking moors and heavy hills. It was a popular tourist route and although the schools were back at work the tourist season still lingered as childless families took advantage of the lower rates. Traffic was thin but steady.

'Take my mobile phone again,' Douglas said. 'At the first sign of any kind of trouble phone Honeypot. She can contact Ziegler for us and she has enough clout to get even the SAS out if she thinks it's necessary. Just key in one-eight six and tell whoever answers where we are and what's happening to us.'

They travelled in silence for some miles. Tash nursed the phone on her lap. The car had a good radio, probably more valuable than the car itself. They listened to the news, none of it very newsworthy, and turned it off.

'If that was some innocent van driver who happened to be in the wrong place at the wrong time,' she said suddenly, 'we'd have heard by now. It would have been all over the news. Anyway, a camper makes a lot of sense. He could watch for us and be on our tails immediately. He couldn't stay in a hotel while the police are looking for him – I mean, even if they don't take the threat to us as seriously as Honeypot does, the least they could do would be to phone around the hotels and boarding houses, but he has to sleep somewhere and the weather isn't settled enough for him to sleep out of doors, except maybe in his car. I'm sure that was him in the camper van.'

'I agree. You're probably right. I hope you are; I'd hate to find that I'd shot up the bread van. I've been trying to think what I'd do if I was in his shoes. Not that I could be in his shoes,' Douglas said absently. Most of his mind was on keeping the car on the road. 'I don't have enough hate in me.'

'Try to imagine really, really hating somebody.'

'I think I'd walk into a caravan dealer's yard and drive out in a motor caravan. But I think he'd have been safe enough in a hotel if he'd changed his appearance a bit. He might have been using a tent.' As he spoke, they saw a small tent on the further side of the stream that followed the broad valley of the Clunie Water. A motorcycle and sidecar stood beside the tent and a man was frying something over a small spirit stove. Douglas watched the man in his mirror but there was no sign of a firearm.

'Hello, we've lost Ziegler,' he said. 'He'll have turned back to meet his VIP.'

It was left to Tash to break another long silence. 'When you shot at that man yesterday – all right, shot at his windscreen – were you reasoning or going on a hunch or did you see him to recognize or what?'

'A bit of each one of them. But mostly I was alerted by the fact that he was always several vehicles behind us, never following us close enough to be recognized or falling back far enough to risk being cut off and losing us. When he turned onto the same road that we did – and I know that road, it doesn't go *anywhere*, except that it becomes a dirt track across the moors and comes out somewhere around here – it all seemed too much of a coincidence.'

'Well, here comes another one. Would you say that he's had time to replace his windscreen and hand-paint the van?'

'Hellfire! Yes, I think he has.' Douglas frowned at each of his mirrors in turn but they only showed him a tourist coach following. 'I don't see anything.'

'He's behind the bus, which is keeping well back. A cream coloured van. It doesn't have the smooth shine of a proper paint job. He could have painted over the windows. He's been ducking back behind the coach so that you only get to see him on bends. A bit late in the year for tourist coaches, isn't it?'

'Not if they're looking for the blue grouse. Very smart if he's got back on our trail already.'

'I may be quite wrong.'

'I hope you are, this time. I don't want a repeat of yesterday's fun and games.'

'I'd rather that we were wrong on the safe side. We only have Honeypot's word for it that he blames us for his downfall and wants blood. But don't forget that he has his sources of information and he was living under the same roof for yonks and we were all more or less swapping CVs. He must know our intentions.'

The car's steering was so slack that Douglas dared not even shrug. 'He could have bribed somebody to phone him if we showed up at the sheltered housing complex. Or he could have got his friend in the garage to fit a what-d'you-call-it device before handing over the car. Tracker, that's the name.'

'There's another sign for Straloch Moor,' Tash said.

'It's the other end of the road we were on yesterday. Phone Honeypot and give her our position by the Satnav.'

TWENTY-FOUR

The side-road arrived before Douglas was quite ready for it – a tarred B-road looking as though it would be passable to the far end. But Douglas had seen the far end and he was doubtful. However, he did not feel that there would be much protection or deterrence in passing traffic or a busload of twitchers. Better perhaps to get off the main road to where he could try to stall things until official help arrived. At a pinch he could ram the coach, immobilize it and drive the car, however damaged, somewhere else before abandoning it.

The one manoeuvre of which the car was still capable was rounding a corner – it was following a straight line that had become difficult. A twitch of the wheel, a yelp from the tyres and they were round and away.

Douglas watched his mirrors. He expected the coach to travel on and the cream caravan to turn in pursuit of them. The caravan driver thought the same and followed patiently. Only when the coach signalled a turn did the caravan suddenly spurt forward, lights flashing and the horn attempting to blare but only managing a dispirited beep. He was too late. The coach was beginning its turn and the caravan had to go on, stop and back up, to the dismay of other traffic. Douglas returned his full attention to his own road just in time to avoid leaving it for the ditch. He put on what speed he could but the road was narrow, single-track with passing places and running through mixed heather that was losing its colour and patches of reedy grass that suggested boggy ground.

'Surely this car should be faster than a camper van?' Tash said. 'Couldn't we just run away and leave them behind?'

'You're right, it should. But you're wrong, it isn't – if only because it has less ground clearance. I haven't been over this road for many years, and nor by the look of it has anybody else, but it doesn't seem to have changed. It's only surfaced for a kilometre or two at each end to give access. The middle bit is only fit for a tractor. There are obstructions that aren't signposted until you get to them. There are boulders that could knock our sump off.'

He put his foot down, ignored the bumps and rattles. He could understand why the last owner had traded in the car and he cursed himself for choosing it unseen from a list. Seymour McLeish would have committed an offence if the car had been resold without an extensive overhaul. The steering had a great deal of play, the suspension was shot and the brakes would have been inadequate on a kiddie's tricycle. In the mirror he saw that the bus had turned to follow him and the camper van, leaving its overtaking manoeuvre too late, had turned behind it.

'It must be a coachload of twitchers,' Tash said. 'He's trying to get by but he doesn't have a hope.'

While he drove and thought and struggled with a road that seemed to have been designed by a deranged goat, he could hear occasional snatches of Tash's voice as she spoke again on the phone. 'Cream motor caravan, registration . . . can't make out the . . . flashing his lights at the coach driver . . . doesn't want to know.' Call finished, she left the phone, still connected, above the dashboard. 'She says to look out for ourselves.'

'I would guess,' Douglas said huskily, 'that that's a hint to defend ourselves as best we can and she'll support a plea of self-defence if it goes that far. My two shotguns are behind the cases. They're already out of their bags but they're open for safety's sake. And they're loaded so don't put your fingers near the triggers; and keep the muzzles down or the cartridges will fall out. Prepare to hand me the over-under. And take a few cartridges out of my left hand pocket and put them into your own.'

'I don't know anything about—'

'Yes you do. You loaded for me at the clay pigeons when we went to Strathbogie. Do the same again. Don't touch the triggers or the safety catches unless you desperately need to shoot.'

'I'll try.' Her voice was shaking but she was still game. He heard the clunk as each gun was closed. His own voice had seemed to be coming from his throat.

There was a change ahead and as a practiced surveyor Douglas took it in in the blink of an eye. Their road was running with a steep escarpment of loose rocks rising on the right. The history was written in the stones. An old road had run straight along the bottom of the escarpment. There had been a rock fall and traffic, mostly of sheep, had become diverted around it through the heather. When the road had been surfaced the new route was followed. Later, the road had gained importance or a roads surveyor had been left with money in his budget that would be lost if it remained unspent, so the original route had been rescued from under the fallen rocks. As a result there was now a D-shape of roads with a rock pile in the middle. Local authorities being ever opportunistic, the place was now adorned with a large P-sign and a picnic symbol. There was even a timber structure forming a table and two cramped double benches.

Sometimes thought can freeze, sometimes it moves with the speed of light. This thankfully was one of the latter occasions. Douglas growled, 'Hang on!' He spurted between the rock walls, stamped on the brakes and hauled the steering round. A dab at the accelerator and the still vigorous engine kicked the tail round. The car stalled to a halt where the roads rejoined. He found himself looking past a shoulder of the rock pile.

The coach driver saw the chance of a respite. His

sandwiches were calling and his passengers had as much chance of seeing a blue grouse there as further on. He swung into the opening of the D, perhaps two cricket pitches from Douglas, but the bend was too tight for his big vehicle and there was a patch of green bog right in front of him. His tail end was blocking the junction. He would have reversed but the camper van had come up close behind, lights flashing and horn sounding. The coach driver opened his door, probably intending to try the use of sweet reason, but the camper driver was not in reasonable mood. A figure roughly conforming to that of George Eastwick jumped out of the camper, carrying a deer rifle complete with telescopic sight, and threw itself down in the shelter of one of the coach's wheels. The coach driver closed his door again and was seen no more.

The car was dangerously exposed. 'Come on!' Douglas snapped. He grabbed his choice of the shotguns, threw open his door, jumped out and ran the three or four paces into the shelter of the rocks. Out of the corner of his eye he saw a slim figure which could only be that of Tash leaping out of the car. He peered through a dip between two boulders and ducked hurriedly, much too late, as a bullet smacked off the stone and whined off into the sky. Chips of stone stung his face. He reckoned to have a second and possibly more while the rifle was reloaded. He raised himself and took a snap shot but he was only shooting at a wheel. If the tyre had suddenly deflated the man might have been pinned down by the weight of the coach; but the resilience of the inflated tyre bounced the small shot off.

At the moment when the world went mad, Douglas was computing the balance of power between himself and George Eastwick. A rifle can kill at a far greater range but it has to be aimed and then reloaded. Only a skilled rifleman can hold his aim while reloading. A shotgun need only be pointed by reflex. It is fitted to the user so that it shoots where he is looking and its pattern has some spread so that if aimed within a very few degrees it should score a hit. Douglas's guns each had twin barrels, allowing an immediate second shot, but a shotgun's range is limited. With ordinary shot, the limit of useful range would be about forty yards. With the heavier SSK shot, which he had only kept in his cupboard in case roe deer came looking for an easy meal among the carnations, the range would be greater, but how much greater he could only hope and guess. He thought that George Eastwick was just within range of a damaging but probably not lethal shot.

He was just arriving at that hasty but comforting conclusion when he was jerked back to the here and now. He had raised his head just enough to see over a ridge of rock. George Eastwick had wriggled sideways to have a clear shot and he was taking aim. Douglas ducked as a second bullet whined off the rock and peppered him with splinters of stone. He snapped off a shot in reply but had no way of knowing whether he had scored. He reloaded. He was relieved that he was holding his over-under clay pigeon gun which had had its safety catch removed. That made for speedier reloading but he would not have wanted to let Tash loose with it.

The scene had settled into a semblance of peace. Douglas used this interval to resume his calculations. One rifle against two shotguns. The rifle would be slower to aim after reloading. In George's shoes, assuming that the open sights were still in place beneath, he would rip off the telescopic sight which would only be an embarrassment at such close range. But Tash had never . . . Douglas suddenly realized that Tash had vanished. This was another new factor in the equation. Had she run for it? Is so, which way?

The passenger door of the bus opened and figures began to pour out. Figures with binoculars and cameras and notebooks and pencils.

Twitchers.

Japanese twitchers.

At the time he could only assume that either he was hallucinating or these twitchers were insane. Later he learned that an Aberdeen firm had seized the chance to advertise trips to see the blue grouse, starting from Dyce Airport, and had come to an arrangement with a travel firm to assemble a complete package of flights, hotels and meals. He also learned that opinion among the twitchers had been divided, some assuming that they had happened on a film in the making, others believing that they had stumbled on a paintball contest.

They began to take photographs, of the scenery and of Douglas and George. One keen photographer crouched down in front of George in order to get a head-on shot, in the photographic sense of the word, of a rifleman taking aim. George was shouting something, inaudible in the babble of Oriental language. This shot was later syndicated worldwide.

Douglas's imaginary scenarios were now scrambled. George, he thought, was in no mood to be deterred from shooting merely by the risk of an innocent Japanese bystander being in the way, but the photographer was mirroring his every move. If Douglas had had the rifle there were moments when he could have fired, but the spread of shot from a shotgun was far too great to be risked in such a crowd. His thinking was becoming disjointed. A moving target is very difficult to hit with a rifle bullet. If Tash came into danger he would jump up and charge.

The photographer had satisfied his urge to capture the dramatic scene. He rose and stepped aside. Again Douglas had to snatch his head out of the way; for a moment he saw George against a background of heather and sky. He had the chance of a shot in reply. The sound of the ricochet and the spatter of shot rebounding into the throng conveyed at last the message that something real was happening in which it might be unwise to become involved.

An unhurried, sheep-like drift towards the door of the coach resulted. George's chance of a clear shot came and went too quickly to be grasped. Douglas got up and darted to one side, to where a ditch and two large stones offered better cover and a better chance of a shot. One snap shot from the rifle missed, high overhead. George felt exposed for an instant and was then safe in cover.

A small cluster of twitchers remained, drifting between George and Douglas. George raised the rifle. He seemed to have turned his head to one side. Douglas assumed that he was looking at Tash. He made his decision, right or wrong. He jumped up again, hurdled the rock and began a desperate charge. Tash, for her part, guessed that George was aiming another shot at Douglas. She had crept round the other side of the coach and was coming up behind George. She changed her grip on Douglas's much prized game gun and arrived behind George already swinging it like a golf club. It was her intention to knock George's head clean off his shoulders and possibly over the crest of the escarpment.

All this Douglas saw. He also saw the muzzle of the rifle settle between his eyes. The barrels of the shotgun caught George across the head and with the jolt of it the shotgun fired. The slam of the shotgun blast coincided with the sharper crack of the rifle so that they could have been mistaken for a single shot.

Douglas saw the quick flicker of flame at the muzzle but he only knew half of the monstrous blow on his head.

The barrels of the gun were damaged beyond repair. So also was George.

Over the brow of the hill came a police car in livery with a coat of arms on the door. Inside were a stout male officer and a young female one, each a constable, each in uniform and neither of them armed. It was, Douglas said later, typically British underkill.

From atop the pile of rocks a single blue grouse looked over the scene and took flight, wondering what was going on. It was not used to being ignored.

TWENTY-FIVE

Pain. Sickness. Smell of disinfectant.
Open eyes but can't see. Kisses on the uncovered part of face and a faint perfume. Cold. Too tired to move. Drumbeat. A familiar voice talking, giving the latest news.

Travelling head first face up. Light and dark. Voices. Needles. Face uncovered, ring of faces, one of them remarkably like Honeypot's and one like Tash. Covered up again. Echoes. Left the road. Rocks among the heather. Head hurts but hallucinations drown the pain. Driving the Ford but too fast to control. Own little BMW much better.

Pipe, tube, hose.

Unwrapping again. Light hurts. Visitors. Yoo who? Mustn't laugh. Hurts. Clay pigeons blowing to dust, gets in your eyes. Pudding club. Shall I be Daddy? Smile when I'm shouting at you.

One second Douglas was wandering in the distant recesses of his mind, the next he was in a hospital bed, desperately cold, being leaned over. The male figure was the surgeon. He didn't know how he knew that; in fact he didn't even know how he knew that it was male. It asked him how many fingers it was holding up. He said that he was too tired to count but that he wasn't seeing double, which seemed to satisfy the figure. Astonishingly, although his memory was patchy his thinking processes were almost too clear.

'He seems to be coming round at long last,' it said. 'It's probably down to you. Keep talking to him. I'll look in again later. I'll send a nurse.'

The figure moved away and was replaced by Tash. She settled in the bedside chair. 'You've done something different with your hair,' he said.

The effect was immediate. Tash emitted a low wail, tears hopped onto her cheeks and she searched in vain for a handkerchief before grabbing a corner of the sheet to mop her nose. 'Are you all right?' she asked in a muffled voice. 'No, that was silly. I know you're not all right but you're going to be. We've been waiting for you to come out of it.'

'I'm cold. Awfully, terribly cold. I'm not dead, am I?'

Tash was trying to laugh and cry at the same time. 'No, you're not dead. But you're still on a transfusion. You lost a terrible lot of blood.'

'But are you all right? How's the baby?'

'He's doing very well.'

'He? How do you know that?'

'They gave me a scan here when they were doing yours. We could see his little spout. I'm calling him Teapot for the moment.'

'Be careful; that kind of nickname can stick.' His head did not seem able to move but by forcing his eyes as high as they would go he saw that there were several bags hanging on a stand and tubes coming down to him. 'Do they take the blood straight out of the fridge and shoot it into you? Tell them to warm it first.' He tried not to sound peevish but without success.

'I'll tell them but I don't suppose they'll listen. It probably gets too thick to flow or something, I'll ask them to give you more blankets. Do you remember what happened?'

'Bits. But I've been dreaming all sorts of dreams and I don't know where they take over. I remember visiting my mother. That was real?'

'Yes. She wrote me a sweet letter.'

Mrs Young was inclined to put off letter writing. And then the post . . .

'How long have I been in here?'

'Just over a week. Go on about how much you remember.'

'There was a coach following us and a camper van behind it. We thought whatshisname – George Eastwick, was it? – might be in the camper. They both turned off when we did. After that I'm not sure . . .'

She put a slim finger to his lips. 'Don't struggle to remember. They say you just have to relax and let it come when it comes. I'll tell you all you need to know. Yes, we thought it was probably George. I don't know why we were so sure, but we were right. You whizzed ahead and swung round and he stopped behind the bus and you fired at him. And he shot at you. Well, I wasn't having that. I went round the back of the coach and came up behind him and he was just taking another shot at you and I wasn't quite quick enough. I swatted him with the barrels of your gun. I'm afraid I bent it badly, do you mind an awful lot?'

'Not in the least. Anyway, it's insured. Take it in to . . .' He ground to a halt, quite unable to remember the name of his usual gun shop.

'No problem, I just filed a receipt from them. So that's all right.' Tash looked deep into his eyes to see whether he was strong enough to discuss his own condition. Her voice became husky with emotion. 'His bullet could have killed you but it ran round between your skull and your scalp; Honeypot says that they do that sometimes. Anyway, I thought he'd killed you and I was just going to do something awful to his body when a police car turned up, the result of my phone call to Honeypot. I thought I might be in trouble—'

'But you're not?'

'No. You see, all the Japanese twitchers—'

'The Japanese . . .?'

'Birdwatchers. The coach was full of them, all with cameras, looking for the blue grouse. There were several video cameras and their what-d'you-call-ems, clips, were all over the TV news next day. They make it quite clear that he'd fired first and I think Honeypot had told the world that George was after your blood, because the papers had some of the photos with headlines referring to him as "assassin".' She paused and looked at her watch. 'We'd better be quick – they want me to keep talking to you but they only let me in during visiting hours, did you ever hear of anything so silly? But it lets me spend hours at your desk. After all the publicity, work keeps rolling in and most of them say that it can wait until you're better, and at least I can do the preliminaries for you. And, listen, do you know what you were talking about while they kept you anaesthetized because of your head injury?'

'No idea,' Douglas said. 'I seemed to dream about all sorts of weird things.'

'Honeypot's delighted. She says you're her golden boy and you can park on a yellow line any time you like. It seems that you solved the last bit of the Stan Eastwood case for her.'

'I did?'

'Yes. You remember, we had it all figured out but there was no proof at all. But you kept babbling about pipes.'

'It was the bagpipes I was dreaming about. A nightmare.'

'I told Honeypot you'd kept mentioning the pipes and she realized that they'd never found the pipe that George had used to pipe the gas in through the wall. And they remembered that he'd been doing some work for a lady who lives next to Seymour's garage. They'd been putting in a ventilator from an internal room through a fan and coming out under the eaves and they found a piece of the flexible ventilation pipe with clear signs of having been pushed into a hole in a stone wall. She says that the forensic scientists have positively matched the dust on it with the stone and mortar of the house.'

Douglas had been waiting for a chance to ask a very important question but he knew that as long as she was sitting at his bedside the question was not urgent. However, at this point Tash fell silent, so he said, 'Then I take it that George is in custody?'

Tash shook her red head. 'Oh no.'

All Douglas's fears came rushing back. 'If George is walking around loose, I don't like the idea of you sleeping at home. I want you well out of harm's way.'

Tash laughed and squeezed his hand. 'He isn't walking around anywhere, silly. When I hit him with the barrels of your gun the gun went off with the shock of it, Honeypot says they quite often do that. It took half his head off. He's as dead as the dodo and I can't say that I'm sorry – a man who would spy on my mum and kill his own brother and come chasing after us. His son seems all right, though, and doesn't seem to be missing his dad at all. The two policemen who turned up were going to get quite stuffy about it but Honeypot turned up a few minutes later and she said that it was perfectly all right. She didn't quite say that I had her permission to knock his block off, but that's how she came over. I'm in some sort of custody but out on bail. She says it will be all right.'

'How do you know George's son?' Douglas asked. His head was beginning to swim, but whether that was due to his injury or to Tash's tendency to leap from subject to subject he could not be sure.

'He's been visiting. Apparently he inherits his father's flat and he likes it much better than the grotty cottage that he's living in just now. Mr Farlane, who owns most of the land around us, was advertising for a keeper, so he thinks he'll go after the job and move in to the granny flat. And he enjoys gardening, isn't that great?'

'He must be off his trolley,' Douglas said. Sleep was crawling over him again. Tash's voice became a mere whisper in the distance. She would have regrets later. He must hurry and recover, get home and be ready to support her if she ever felt guilty.

Douglas woke up again suddenly. 'He may be tarred with the same brush as his father and his uncle. Get an electrician to come in and rip out the wiring.'